If you are only able to read large print, you may qualify for Wolfner Library services which include free access by mail to:

- Over 350,000 titles in audio and other formats
- Use of audio playback devices
- DVDs with descriptive narration
- Over 70 audio magazines

**Wolfner Talking Book and Braille Library**

Email: Wolfner@sos.mo.gov
Toll free: 800-392-2614 (in Missouri)
Phone: 573-751-8720

# No Mercy

# NO MERCY

## Jack Curtis

**Thorndike Press • Chivers Press**
**Thorndike, Maine USA    Bath, Avon, England**

This Large Print edition is published by Thorndike Press, USA and by Chivers Press, England.

Published in 1996 in the U.S. by arrangement with Walker Publishing Company, Inc.

Published in 1996 in the U.K. by arrangement with Walker and Company.

| U.S. | Hardcover | 0-7862-0704-3 | (Western Series Edition) |
| U.K. | Hardcover | 0-7451-4862-X | (Chivers Large Print) |
| U.K. | Softcover | 0-7451-4868-9 | (Camden Large Print) |

All the characters and events portrayed in this work are fictitious.

Thorndike Large Print ® Western Series.

The text of this Large Print edition is unabridged.
Other aspects of the book may vary from the original edition.

Set in 16 pt. News Plantin by Minnie B. Raven.

Printed in Great Britain on permanent paper.

British Library Cataloguing in Publication Data available

Library of Congress Cataloging in Publication Data

Curtis, Jack, 1922–
   No mercy / Jack Curtis.
     p.    cm.
    ISBN 0-7862-0704-3 (lg. print : hc)
    1. Large type books.  I. Title.
  [PS3505.U866N6    1996]
  813'.54—dc20
                                       96-12105

*For*
*Robert A. Hamilton*

# CHAPTER 1

"Oh, the buckaroo loves the whistle of
      his rope
As he gallops over the plains . . . ."

Clint Durby's voice stretched close to unraveling. The heel of his right boot stomped the saloon's already scarred pine floor. His rope-callused left hand kept time, banging on the bar, while his right hand tipped his wide-brimmed hat back, revealing a white stripe between his sun-blackened forehead and his straight black hair.

"And the stage driver loves the popper of
      his whip
And the rattle of his Concord chains . . . ."

His wide-spaced gray eyes were nearly closed as he bayed at the pressed-tin ceiling and his generous mouth strained into a grinning megaphone.

"And I pray the Lord we'll all be saved
And we'll keep the golden rule . . . ."

Lee, his blond look-alike younger brother, smiled and winked at Salty Salkeld, the bartender, whose stubbled features revealed a crusty displeasure emphasized by his muttering, "Dang screech owl . . ."

"But I'd rather be in bed with my
      yellow-haired gal
Than kiss the butt of a goddamned mule!"

A young puncher named Blackie, dozing in the corner of the saloon, his boots up on a wired-together chair and his head tilted back against the flyspecked wall, snorted and pawed at his ear, then resumed his nap.

Another uncaring puncher sat at a table, playing solitaire, not cheating until he knew it was hopeless.

Other cowboys wearing spurs, leather leggings, and vests, stared at the mirror behind the bar, sipping their beer, waiting for something to happen.

"Daggone it, Lee —" Clint Durby looked around at the shadowed, silent room. "I swear this is one of them wax-museum places where nobody talks or so much as wiggles an eyebrow. They just hang up their saddles, swaller their tongues, and accumulate dust."

No one paid attention to the tall cowboy. The Regulator clock on the wall tick-tocked slowly. A fly buzzed against the window. "Everybody but you has growed up, big brother." Lee smiled, his young face unlined by sun or wind, his eyes wide open from city living as compared to the tight squint of Clint's eyes that served as a protection against driving dust or sleet, alkali or sun glare.

"Growed up and turned into tombstones," Clint protested. "What's the matter with folks just havin' fun?"

"The West is too civilized for that now," Lee replied, teasing. "How are you going to climb the ladder of success, acting like a clown all the time?"

"If I got to act like a danged bogged-down doughbelly, I'm not goin' anywhere." Clint shook his head and glared at the silent, apathetic customers. "Hell, I used to be an honest cowhand, now I'm more a nurse for high-toned dudes."

"It's just for another week, Clint," Lee said encouragingly. "Soon as they go back east, you can go back to kissin' cows."

"Hell's fire, I'm ashamed to look a real cow in the face," Clint said, laughing. "Maybe I ought to drive a herd of Longhorns by His Lordship's shooting stand and see how many he knocks down with his Big Fifty before he figures out he's shootin' at his own beef 'stead of deer and elk!"

"I'll be going east myself in a couple of weeks," Lee said absently, running a length of soft leather lacing between his fingers. He was studying in Chicago to be a newspaper reporter. "How you going to get along without your little brother keeping you out of trouble?"

"That's different," Clint said. "You're goin' to be educated and bring in some money."

"Don't count on it," Lee said, grinning. "Journalists are worse than cowboys when it comes to making money."

"At least you'll know somethin'," Clint argued. "That's more than I can say for myself."

"Amen to that," Salty muttered, swabbing the bar. And to Lee he said directly, "Don't worry about this crazy cuss, kid. You get on with your schooling."

"I don't need no guardian," Clint snorted. "Give me that string. I'll bet you a dime I can throw Blackie into the corner without even touchin' him."

Lee pushed a dime out to cover his brother's and said, "Not too hard."

Taking the leather, Clint moved over to the sleeping cowboy, looked his length up and down, then leaned over and tied the thong around the shanks of his spurs.

Taking a chair near Blackie's reclining head, Clint picked up a deck of cards from the table and drawled conversationally to the sleeping cowboy, "Yes, sir, there are some big sidewinders around here. Biggest rattlesnakes I ever seen . . . Some of 'em six feet long. Gray and brown, black, or diamondback, they're always movin'. Prairie rattlers, timber rattlers, sand rattlers, big as your leg, with fangs full of poison . . ."

The sleeping young puncher's head shifted slightly as Clint murmured in his ear.

Gripping the deck of cards with his left hand, Clint continued his monotone, "Comes a time one of them big timber rattlers slips into your bedroll, creepin' in slow and deadly, and curls up on your chest, and opens his jaws wide . . ."

Holding the deck of cards near Blackie's ear, Clint ripped his heavy thumbnail down over the end of the cards, creating a loud, rapid clatter.

Blackie's eyes bulged in terror and his mouth formed a silent scream as he dove for the door, but the leather thong sent him crashing into the corner.

Clint strolled back to the bar, nodded at Lee, and moved the two dimes over to his side. "Just like a dang rooster with his head chopped off."

"Damn it, Clint!" Blackie yelled. "Why can't you let a man get some rest!"

11

"You can rest in heaven." Clint smiled. "Why sleep your life away?"

"Well, I know where you're goin', and they don't get no rest down there," Blackie grumbled, undoing the lacing from his spurs and going back to his chair.

The room returned to its former ticktock tranquility despite Clint's attempt to liven up the day.

Impatiently striding back and forth before the bar, Clint looked past Salty at the back counter, where a glass jar of pickled pig's feet stood alongside another jar of pickled eggs that looked unappetizingly like rolled-up eyeballs in the cloudy vinegar.

Next to the jars was a bowl full of plain brown eggs, a block of rat cheese covered by a towel, and two round loaves of bread, all of them makings for the free lunch.

"Give me one of them boiled eggs, Salty," Clint said, "and some salt."

"Them eggs ain't ready," Salty replied. "I haven't had time to boil 'em yet."

"Give me one anyway," Clint said.

"You want me to crack it in your beer?" Salty grumbled.

"No, Mister Bar Dog." Clint smiled. "I just want to educate you."

"If it's makin' an egg stand up in a mound of salt, I already seen it."

"Bet you a dime, Salty, I can make it stand up on its hind end without using any salt."

"I just doubt you can even make your tallywhacker stand up without whippin' it with a willow switch," Salty growled, passing over an egg.

"He don't have a dime, little brother, just rough talk. You got a dime's worth of sportin' blood in you?"

"You going to make that egg stand on end without using salt, sawdust, or suchlike?" Lee asked tolerantly before pushing over another dime.

"I am, or die tryin'. Anybody else want to get in on this high-stakes lesson?" Clint addressed the drowsy room, then added, "Them boys is ponderin' so hard they don't have time to think."

"You goin' to do your trick, or you just goin' to jabber on like a jackass eatin' cactus?" Blackie yelled from the other side of the room.

"Very well, boys, Chris Columbus used salt," Clint chuckled, "but us cowboy pistoleros use a gun."

Drawing his Colt .44, Clint pointed it at the ceiling, then set the egg end on the muzzle of the gun, his hand unwavering.

"Satisfied?" Clint grinned at Salty.

"Give me back that egg before you drop it," Salty growled, holding out his open hand.

"That's a pretty good trick, big brother." Lee smiled. "Got any more?"

"One more." Clint chuckled, his eyes merry, ignoring Salty's outstretched hand.

Taking the egg with his left hand, he tossed it into the air and caught it gently, then tossed it again, higher this time.

"Don't," Salty grated.

When, on the third throw, the egg lofted almost as high as the ceiling, Clint drew the Colt swiftly and fired, splattering the egg as well as making a significant hole through the pressed tin.

Punchers moved aside as the shattered egg dripped from the ceiling.

"Out!" Salty roared. "Outside, and don't come back!"

"Me?" Clint asked innocently, holstering the smoking .44.

"Yes, you! You! You!" Salty grabbed a short-barreled shotgun from under the bar, his eyes blazing. "Always playin' the fool! Well, no more! I don't have to put up with your idiot pranks, and that's final!"

"Yessir," Clint said, hunching his shoulders, spreading his hands, and backing toward the door. "I did wake 'em up, though —"

"I'll be along after a while, big brother . . ." Lee opened a cardboard-bound notebook on the bar and commenced writing. "I want to record your demonstration for posterity."

"Heck, a man can't even have a little fun anymore," Clint grumbled. "I'll bet you a dime I can hit six eggs all in one throw."

"Out!" Salty roared, his face flushed with anger, his voice cracking. "And don't come back to the Calico Queen until you're as growed-up as your little brother."

Clint backed out the door onto the boardwalk, shaking his head, muttering. "Growed-up? Who wants to be growed-up?"

"What's that all about?" came a harsh voice.

Clint turned to face the sheriff, a man with faded eyes and a grizzled bar of a mustache over an unsmiling mouth. His once broad shoulders were humped forward, and pinned on his cowhide vest was a brass star.

"Somebody target-practicing, Earl," Clint said easily. "It's too dangerous in there for me."

"There was just one shot," Sheriff Earl Cox said, peering over the batwing doors, observing the peaceable room, and looking back at Clint. "Your doin'?"

"Not me, Sheriff. I just come in from the ranch to buy sarsparilla for our three sportsmen." Clint smiled. "We just hog that stuff down from huntin' so hard."

"Never serious, are you?" The sheriff shook his head bleakly. "If I have to put you in jail

15

tonight, I'm not turnin' you loose for a week."

Looking over Sheriff Cox's hunkered shoulders, Clint saw a young lady wearing an ankle-length red-and-yellow-striped dress. Her piled-up hair was pure black and topped by a round lacquered yellow straw hat with an egret feather.

Ruby Campbell's face was a mixture of young and old. Without powder and rouge, her skin looked pale and sallow, unused to sunlight. Her young mouth was already defeated, her old eyes downcast as she came along the boardwalk.

Two ladies dressed in gray, walking the other way, shuddered and froze into rigid postures, their noses going up like a pair of hounds downwind of a polecat. As they passed the garishly dressed sporting girl, they lifted the hems of their dresses an inch as if wading through fresh cowplop, glancing back over their shoulders with hateful contempt.

The girl flinched as they passed, and kept her eyes down on the boardwalk.

"Afternoon, Miss Ruby." Clint raised his hat. "You're lookin' pretty as a little red heifer in a flower bed today."

Glancing up swiftly at him, she murmured, "Afternoon, Clint."

"What the blazes?" the sheriff growled, his head jerking around to get a look at her.

16

"What are you doing uptown?"

"I'm aimin' to buy some medicine," Ruby replied weakly.

"Just a minute, girl —" Sheriff Cox caught her by the arm. "You know the laws — nauchtown women don't trespass uptown."

"I know, Sheriff," Ruby said, her voice resigned. "But Miss Kitt is awful sick, and Doc Snordt won't come down for less'n five dollars."

"It don't make no nevermind." The sheriff kept his hold on her arm. "You just turn around, and go right back where you come from," the sheriff said bluntly. "You know your place and I know my job."

"Miss Kitt is like to die . . . ," Ruby said, turning away, her eyes on the boardwalk. "There's nobody down there to help. I wouldn't have come if she didn't need medicine real bad."

"It ain't my doin'," the sheriff said, releasing her arm. "Folks make the rules, I just enforce them. If I don't, they'll get somebody else who will, and I'm too old to start lookin' for another job just because some old bawd thinks she's sick."

"Yes, sir," Ruby murmured. "I don't want to cause no trouble."

"It's no trouble, Ruby," Clint said, easing in front of Sheriff Cox and crooking his right arm. "I'll be glad to walk you up to the mercantile."

"No, Clint. You heard —"

"Ruby, it's a public boardwalk," Clint said easily. "That means anybody can walk on it, because one way or another we're all payin' for it."

"Durby, you're just beggin' for trouble today, ain't you?" the sheriff said, frowning.

"I'm escortin' my lady friend to the store. We're goin' to spend some money for the medicine, then we'll go back down to nauchtown and doctor a sick lady. Is there a law against that?"

"There damned well is and you know it. None of them crosses the gulch. That's the law!"

"Let's change the law then, since it don't sound fair," Clint said, grinning. "Let's change it so the ladies uptown can walk down through nauchtown and the ladies of nauchtown can walk through uptown."

"You'd have them pickin' up the cowboys right here in broad daylight, wouldn't you, Durby?"

"We're just sayin' anybody can go anywhere, whether it's for business or pleasure. 'Course, them that wants to do business with Miss Ruby have to go down to her shop."

"Don't make this any worse with your foolishness, Durby," the sheriff threatened, his jaw set. "The law is the law."

"No trouble, Clint," Ruby said. "I'm leavin'."

"Now, Ruby, you got to figure you're just as good as anybody else in this town, no matter how they treat you," Clint said with a smile. "Otherwise, there wouldn't be most of the male population down there after dark."

"Goldurn it, Durby" — the sheriff moved in front of Ruby and faced the tall cowboy head-on — "you always have to play the fool. Law means nothin' to you."

"There's laws and laws." Durby smiled. "Laws for the rich, laws for the poor."

"That ain't none of your business," the sheriff blustered. "Lawin' is my business. If it means havin' to lock you up, I'll sure do it."

"I reckon you'd try if you thought you could," Clint said mildly. "But just now me and Miss Ruby's goin' to go buy some medicine."

"Have it your way." The sheriff sighed, and looking beyond Clint, he nodded. "Go ahead, buffalo the idjit."

Before Clint could turn, a heavy revolver barrel landed above his right ear, and Clint crumpled like a coldcocked bull, his last thought being that he should have been listening instead of talking.

Ruby scurried back down the street with an unladylike haste and didn't stop until she'd reached the gulch.

Poor damn fool, she thought, getting her breath back. So damn sweet, but so damn foolish too. . . .

Deputy Henry Arbuckle, a lean, cadaverous man with a spiky mustache, holstered the .44 and said, "Suit you?"

"No," Cox said. "Now I have to put up with his nonsense for a week."

"I got to feed him," Arbuckle said with equal resentment.

With each man taking a shoulder, they dragged Clint Durby down the boardwalk to the jail, his boot toes vibrating over the cracks in the boards.

Unbuckling Durby's gunbelt, the sheriff let Arbuckle close the iron-barred door and turn the key.

"He said there was laws and laws — like I don't already know that. Anyway, I got tired arguin' with 'im."

Arbuckle nodded and said, "Town folks want the sporters, but they have to pretend they don't."

"They say the sporters keep the cowboys from violatin' their women," the sheriff said, chuckling dryly. "But I never saw a cowboy who'd even want one of *their* women."

Arbuckle forgot what he was going to reply when Lee Durby quietly entered and said, "Afternoon, gents, I understand my brother's taken a room here."

"And you might figure he's goin' to occupy it for the next seven days, too," the sheriff said.

"Hurt bad?" Lee asked, not smiling.

"Not a chance," Arbuckle replied. "I just tapped him an hour's worth, unless he's got a thin skullbone."

"Which he ain't, as I know well enough," the sheriff said. "Come back tomorrow."

"Tell him I'll fill in for him out at Sawtooth," the fresh-faced yellow-haired youth said.

"Think you can handle those dudes?" the sheriff asked, smiling. "Drivin' game, waitin' on 'em hand and foot?"

"Nobody else will volunteer." Lee nodded. "Badger Corbin won't be pleased when Clint doesn't show up."

"They say one of 'em is a duke . . . ?" Arbuckle said.

"Duke of Dorset. Looks about as appealing as a scorpion with his stinger up." Lee smiled. "But compared to the other two, he's a regular cream pie."

"I reckon if you own the biggest ranch in

21

Montana Territory, you don't have to be nice to the hired help," the sheriff said firmly. "Town wouldn't even be here if it wasn't for them and their money."

"As long as they got so much money, it'd be nice if they paid a fair wage," Lee replied.

"A man can always quit and go someplace else," Arbuckle said smugly.

"Just like this town could amount to something if those three hadn't gobbled up half the Crow Reservation," Lee said.

"You learn that radical talk back east, boy?" the sheriff asked coldly. "Maybe you been goin' to the wrong school."

"No offense, gents." Lee held up his hands, palms out, and smiled. "You want to side Sawtooth Syndicate, fine with me."

"I don't side anybody," Sheriff Cox growled. "I'm for law and order, and that's it."

"If you have time, tell Clint I'll see him tomorrow night."

With that, the young man was gone.

Sheriff Cox stirred uncomfortably in his chair. "That's what schoolin' does. Learns 'em disrespect."

"Those three pooh-bahs'll teach him a lesson he won't forget they hear him talkin' about a fair wage," Arbuckle said, then snorted knowingly.

"Sheriff . . . ," came a hollow voice from down the hall.

Arbuckle chuckled. "The clown is wakin' up and lookin' for his head."

"Sheriff . . . , you out there?"

"I'm here," Sheriff Cox retorted loudly, cleaning his fingernails with his jackknife.

"Could I have a drink of water, please, sir?" Clint's voice came back weakly.

"Give him a dipper of water," the sheriff said.

Arbuckle took a pail of water and a long-handled dipper down the hall and let Clint drink through the bars.

"You're goin' to kill a man like that, some-day," Clint said, dropping the dipper back in the pail.

"Not much else I could do, Durby," Arbuckle said. "You bein' so fast with the gun and all."

"I don't shoot people," Durby said. "You could just say 'Go to jail' and I'd do it."

"How could I be sure? A man crazy enough to stand up for a goddamned whore!"

"There's whores and whores. Just like there's laws and laws," Durby said, holding his head with both hands.

"You're wrong, Durby," Arbuckle said firmly. "A whore is a whore and laws is laws."

"They pay you to think that way," Durby

23

murmured weakly, "but deep down you must know better."

The emaciated deputy glared through the bars. "That baby-faced brother of yours come by and says he'll fill in for you tomorrow and be back tomorrow night."

"How much is bail?" Clint asked.

"No bail," the sheriff yelled from the other room. "I aim to learn you somethin'."

"But that ain't the law either. I got a right to bail."

"Not till the judge comes next week," the sheriff replied.

"Hell," Arbuckle said, grinning, "we can keep you in here for a year or two and nobody'd ever know the difference."

# CHAPTER 2

Unused to being confined in an eight-by-eight cell, Clint Durby suffered through the hours of solitude, pacing the floor, back and forth. *I wish I was out of here. I wish I'd never seen this flea-bit company town. I wish I'd ducked. I wish I'd stayed home. I wish I had a home. I wish Lee'd waited till I woke up. I wish Miss Ruby was in here with me. I wish the ocean was whiskey and I was a duck . . .*

Sheriff Cox stayed away, leaving his deputy to bring Clint his meals from Ike's Cafe across the street, and Arbuckle had nothing to say except dumb things like "You goin' to smarten up after a while, boy. Sooner or later, you goin' to learn respect for the law. It don't pay bein' a joker forever. . . ."

*I wish I was out of here. I wish I could go off and marry a rich, deaf and dumb widow woman. I wish I was invisible. I wish I could fly. I wish I was cool as a skunk in the moonlight . . .*

Midafternoon, Sheriff Cox brought Lee down the hall, saying, "The answer is no. He stays in for a week just like I said ten times already."

25

"But Badger will likely fire him if he's off much longer. With the owners looking over his shoulder, Badger can't pass over some things."

"That's your brother's problem, boy. I reckon in about a week it'll sink through his thick head that it don't pay to buck the law," Sheriff Cox said righteously. "It don't mean fiddley-dee to me whether he gets fired or not."

"Begging your pardon, Sheriff," Lee responded politely, "you put him in, you could let him out."

"You got that right, son," the sheriff said, leaving Lee at the cell door.

"You're early," Clint said through the bars. "Got any bail money?"

"Sheriff won't take it, Clint," the youth said. "Judge won't be back from Virginia City for about a week. I guess you made Earl a little scratchy."

"Badger could talk me out. He gets along fine with lawmen."

"Badger's some put out, himself," Lee said. "I was supposed to drive some big deer by the shooting stand this morning, but they spooked when I was working 'em through the pines, and nobody got a shot."

"Hell's fire," Clint said grimly, "cowboys ain't s'posed to herd deer!"

"I don't figure I'm a real cowboy." Lee smiled. "I'm just working my way through college."

"Next thing you know they'll have us cuttin' hay," Clint complained.

"There's something not square about those high-finance dudes," Lee said quietly, hunkering down on his heels.

"They didn't get all the money in the world by bein' square," Clint said. "But that's their business."

"I ran across something," Lee said.

"You tryin' to be a newspaper writer already?" Clint smiled. "First, you better figure either the senator or Big Jim Ralston already owns the newspapers."

"They can't own 'em all, can they?"

"Maybe not, but they're all backscratchin' cousins," Clint said. "What's rawin' you?"

"First those 'valets,' they call them, all look like street fighters I see back in South Chicago. They spend most of their time watchin' the women."

"Stay away from them women, little brother," Clint said. "Them high muck-a-mucks don't want to share nothin' with a thirty-dollar-a-month cowboy."

"There's something doesn't fit," Lee said, shaking his head. "Why do they come out here at all? Most of the time they're just wrangling

27

over their big deals."

"Out here, there's nobody can spy on 'em."

"And why have they taken the trouble to ride clear through the Crow Reservation?"

"It isn't so hard in a surrey with a Cavalry escort," Clint said. "Maybe they're goin' to give the Indians a fair shake for a change."

"Do you believe that?" Lee asked, staring at Clint.

"Never in a pig's patooty." Clint grinned. "But it's their business, not ours."

"I dunno . . . back at school, they talk about democracy and fair play and such stuff. Seems like we all ought to be pulling together."

"That sort of thinkin' will get you in more trouble than stickin' up for a sportin' girl." Clint chuckled.

"Suppose one honest man could make a difference. Suppose Big Jim Ralston went broke? Suppose Senator Lorenzo Cooley was kicked out of office? Suppose the duke was booted out of the country? . . . Even better, suppose all three had to stand public trial before a jury of their peers?"

"I just want to see you finish school," Clint said seriously.

"Something's not right, and it's big," Lee said dreamily. "I'd sure like to catch 'em out . . ."

"You fellers goin' to yammer all day?"

Sheriff Cox yelled from his office.

"He's right, big brother," Lee said. "I got to get back. It's kind of fun playing the detective —"

"Listen to me, Lee. You ain't a detective. You ain't even a newspaperman yet, and them fellers don't ever miss a trick. I want you to leave off, at least until I'm out of here," Clint said strongly, gripping the bars in his big hands, trying to make the kid pay attention.

"I may not be able to get loose to come back for a couple days, big brother, but don't worry about me."

"You ever know me to worry about anything? Only thing on my mind is waltzin' Miss Ruby through the night, restin' my chin betwixt her bosoms." Clint spread his arms to enclose the invisible Miss Ruby, and sashayed around the small cell, kicking up his heels.

"Clint, you'd make the best cattleman in Montana if you ever decide to grow up." Lee smiled and walked down the hall.

"Comin' from you, youngster, that's a danged insult," Clint hooted at his departing brother.

That night, after he'd blown out the lamp and lay back on the single bunk, looking up at the dark ceiling, Clint thought about his early days in Kansas when the two of them were just barefoot country boys trying to help

29

their dad with the plowing or their mama with the butter churn, until he'd discovered what a terrible kind of slavery they'd acquired just by growing up.

Looking at a mule's butt all day while he pulled a plow up and down a rocky field could hardly be called exciting or even meaningful, because every year they seemed to be worse off.

The farm work became even more monotonous and dull after he'd started trading horses, until he had a pretty fair pony all his own. Once he'd felt the majesty of horsemanship, he regarded plowing as labor unworthy of human beings.

He was seventeen when the mule died and Dad gave up. Lee was twelve. Another year and likely Clint would have run off to join a cattle drive north, but as it was, he took a job in the cattle pens in Ellsworth and the rest of the family went back to Chicago, where Dad found work in the packing house, Mama took in sewing, and Lee went to school. That was eight years ago already, he thought, and you're still a clown.

At least Lee will amount to something when he graduates in the spring.

And the kid's even a pretty fair cowboy, considering he only comes out to the ranch three months a year.

Eight years ago Clint had gone out on his own and drifted along with the cattle, picking up a twenty-dollar saddle and a forty-dollar hat along the way, until he'd been hired on by Badger Corbin and took a liking to the great Sawtooth Valley.

Sure, in the winters he sometimes hankered for Matamoros instead of Montana, but then one day you'd see the water seeping out from under the snow and that would mean spring roundup was just around the corner.

You hire on to a ranch for so many years, you get some privileges, so you can take your kid brother to town on a Saturday and look for a good time.

Trouble was, everybody was settling down and didn't like to hoo-raw much anymore. Here I am, twenty-five years old, and everybody looks at me like I should be an old-timer gummin' his pipe and rockin' on the front porch.

Most of the ordinary halfway decent young hands that had been in the bunkhouse when he'd arrived at the Sawtooth were married and gone off somewhere to better-paying, less dangerous work.

It was only the ugly, the halt, the blind, and the clown who hadn't found a lady to settle down with, he thought ruefully.

Trouble was, when it came to marriageable

women, he was all gurgle and no guts. Maybe
seein' Dad fail and Mama go downhill so fast
— it was a mercy their passin' on — kind
of made him spooky about havin' a family and
all.

About all I want to carry on my shoulder
is my saddle, he thought. . . .

Next day, trying to break up the do-nothing
boredom, he tried to balance the half-full
china thundermug on top his head and was
doing pretty good at it until he started waltzing
Miss Ruby around the cell.

Hearing the crash, Sheriff Cox hurried
down the hall, saw the mess, shook his head
grimly, and went back out to his office.

"Ain't you goin' to give me a mop and a
bucket?" Clint yelled after him.

There was no response, and Clint spent the
rest of the afternoon sweeping the floor with
the side of his boot, making a neat pile of
broken china by the iron-barred door.

After that, they gave him a tin bucket instead of a crockery pot.

". . . 'Does the wind blow this way all the
time?' the dude asked," Shorty Hedspeth said
at the end of the day when they were sitting
around the bunkhouse. " 'No, mister,' I said,
'it'll maybe blow this way for a week or ten
days and then it'll change direction and blow

like hell for a while!' "

Shorty laughed at his own joke, and the others who'd heard it often enough chuckled politely.

Sitting on the edge of his bunk in the lamplight, Lee Durby copied off the tale in his notebook as a part of his ongoing collection of cowboy sayings, jokes, yarns, and songs.

"Too bad, Lee." Cooky made a face like a monkey. "I could tell you plenty of jokes, but you couldn't write 'em down for fear of setting your notebook afire."

"Everything fits somewhere." Lee smiled and added, "I'm wonderin' how those hooligan valets fit into this peaceable kingdom."

"Don't pay to wonder overmuch," Blackie said softly. "Especially if you got to work with them tomorrow."

"Never interfere with nothin' that ain't directly botherin' you none," Shorty said.

After a while the maniacal scream of a coyote ripped through the darkness. "Hear that old-dog coyote up on the hill?" Lee asked.

Going to the open door, he listened to the wildness of the predator night and after a moment stepped outside into the yard.

The moon hadn't risen yet, but the massive dome of stars shone through the clear air like a mantle of starched white lace. Off to his left he saw the bulk of the lodge and the yellow lamplight in several of its many windows.

What were they up to now, Lee wondered. A senator, an English nobleman, and a railroad magnate, all getting along like three pups in a basket.

What a story he could write if he just had some evidence of what they were planning.

Strolling across the bare yard toward the huge lodge, he tried to fit together the little suspicious pieces he'd heard and seen, but it was like a bucket with a hole in it — it wouldn't hold water.

Reaching a broad veranda that stood higher than his head, he waited quietly, listening to the ladies laughing and the rumble of men's voices inside.

Suddenly the front door opened, and the veranda was bathed in lamplight as the three men stepped out.

Lee, afraid he'd seem to be spying, moved in close to the front wall where he couldn't be seen unless someone came to the railing and looked straight down.

He smelled the rich aroma of Cuban cigars and the creak of padded lounge chairs as the men took their seats.

"Excellent buffalo hump," the Britisher said, his voice nasal like a sheep blatting.

"The Beaujolais was perfect," the senator

said, his voice trained to carry out over the crowds.

"Great minds need some sustenance." The financier laughed heavily.

"Sending the Crow Indians to Canada is on my mind," the Duke of Dorset murmured.

"And replacing them with our own benevolent enterprises." Senator Cooley chuckled. "Casino, hotel, racecourse . . ."

"More lucrative than benevolent." Big Jim's voice sounded like the growl of a threatened bulldog.

"Quite so," said the Britisher.

"Let's hope there's no last-minute snag," the senator said.

"We'll wind it up as soon as we return to New York," Big Jim said. "There will be no last-minute snags."

"More cognac, Your Lordship?" asked the senator.

"Yes, a spot, please," the Britisher said.

Lee heard the men rise and the clink of a bottle against glasses. Their footsteps moved to the edge of the veranda, and the duke said, "Here's to a really big killing!"

"And here's to more for us and less for them!" The senator laughed.

"We'll show them no mercy," Big Jim said, his voice booming. "Cheers!"

Lee ducked aside as a brandy snifter tum-

35

bled down to the soft ground in front of him.

"Oh, damn, I dropped it," the Britisher said.

Quickly Lee grabbed the fragile globe-shaped glass and lifted it high.

"Here it is," he spoke out cheerfully, knowing he was caught and that he would have to talk fast.

"I got here just in the nick of time," he called up to the three dark shapes on the veranda.

The duke took the glass from Lee's hand and asked, "How long have you been hiding down there?"

"I just now got here, Your Lordship," Lee said quickly. "I came up from the bunkhouse to let you know I'll be taking my brother's place tomorrow."

"You've been listening," the senator said accusingly.

"Yes, sir, I been listening to that old coyote on the hill, nothing else," Lee said.

"I don't like this," Big Jim said slowly. "I won't have my employees sneaking around in the dark."

"It's not my fault the moon's not up yet," Lee said. "I really wasn't sneaking around. I was just trying to do my job."

"What all did you hear?" the Britisher asked.

"I heard someone — talking about the hunt, I suppose — saying 'We'll show them no mercy. Cheers!' " Lee said. "Then I saw the glass falling and the duke said, 'Oh, damn, I dropped it.' "

"Gentlemen," a female voice called from the open doorway, "have you finished your cigars?"

"We'll speak of this tomorrow, young man," Big Jim said to Lee. He turned away from the railing, saying to the ladies waiting at the door, "What's the matter, you girls lonesome for the big bad hunters?"

As Lee turned away, he thought, You're not the only hunters out here, and I'm not finished, not by a long shot . . .

The next day was worse for Clint. Breakfast was day-old rice pudding. Dinner was the usual plate of beans starting to turn sour, and a chunk of weevily bread.

"You boys been raidin' the dog's bowl again, ain't you," Clint said, sniffing at the beans and sliding the plate back outside. He tore the bread into crumbs and put them up on his window ledge, hoping to attract some sparrows for company, but a line of ants formed on the wall and went to work.

Is a thousand ants worth one sparrow? he asked himself, and then thought, Clint Durby, you're goin' plumb loco. He went back to walking the floor by putting one boot exactly ahead of the other, heel to toe, heel to toe, eight times, turn around and do it again.

Midafternoon, he heard voices up the hall in the sheriff's office, then the sheriff came down and unlocked the iron-barred door. His face was set firm and frozen, like a gambler holding a busted flush.

"Come on." He led the way back to the office.

"Judge come back?" Clint asked hopefully.

The lawman didn't answer, but his hunkered-over shoulders seemed to carry some extra weight.

Passing into the office, the sheriff took the heavy oak chair behind his desk to face Badger Corbin, a gray-haired man with the weather-carved features and set expression in his eyes of a rider who'd worked along the frontier for so long he was master of it and the men who'd come after him.

His tied-down holster suggested he might have been a gunman at one time, probably along the Mexican border from his sidewise Texas drawl, and he easily wore the cloak of authority as the boss of the Sawtooth Ranch.

Facing Clint, he looked through his squint eyes at the stubble-faced puncher and drawled, "Got bad news for you, Clint."

"You gettin' me out of that cage is good news to me, Badger," Clint said without thinking. Then, seeing the level gaze of the older man, he asked, "What?"

"Your kid brother. Lee. Had an accident." A harshness graveled his voice, but he held his eyes on Clint's.

"What kind of accident?" Clint asked, dry-mouthed, his empty stomach queasy.

"Was shot this morning. He's dead."

"You ain't jokin' me, are you?" Clint's voice trembled and his vision wavered.

"It's true," Sheriff Cox said. "I went out soon as I heard, to make sure it was accidental."

"But . . . how . . . ?"

"Somehow something happened to his horse. He came walking up toward the shootin' stand with the saddle on his shoulder, they said. It was still hazy dawn and the three of them thought he was a bull elk the way the saddle changed his silhouette.

"Anyways he come crashin' through the trees with that saddle on his shoulder and the three of them cut down on him."

"Oh, Lord," Clint said in a painfully small voice, "he was just a kid . . ."

"I'm sorry," Badger said.

"You're free, Durby," the sheriff said, pushing Clint's gunbelt across the desk. "Your horse is over at the livery."

"Go ahead," Badger Corbin said. "I'll catch up with you."

In a daze, Clint went down to the livery and saddled the long-legged bay. He took the trace west up the long valley that gently curved northward. Twenty miles from town, the headquarters of the Sawtooth Cattle Syndicate would be standing close to the upthrust Sawtooth range where his kid brother lay dead. All the promise, all the effort to be something, all the future that should have been Lee's, now blown down and wasted.

"It should have been me — he was doin' my job while I was playin' the fool. And now there's no changin' it . . . ," he murmured out loud, his eyes wet. "Something like this just couldn't be in the cards, you'd think. Then all of a sudden, somebody calls your hand, turns up the ace of spades, and you've lost the whole shebang, everything you had and everything Lee wanted. And he really wanted something."

It don't seem possible, he thought, keeping the bay moving at a mile-eating canter that wouldn't kill him. How? Why?

Miles before he reached the ranch headquarters, he knew there would be no answer. Not from God, not from the great forested mountains forever hooded with snow, not from the sparkling river coursing down the middle of the rich green valley. Not from the cascade of steaming hot water pouring over a pink and white cliffside, nor from the enormous pale blue sky that went beyond distance into timelessness.

Sawtooth was no simple pioneer outfit scratching out a living raising beef. It had been born rich, and an architect had calculated every detail of the terrain before drawing the plans from the ground up.

The pole fences ran in exact straight lines, their corners square. The great lodge, built of peeled pine logs, stood on a little rise next to an enormous thrust of granite that became a part of a cloud-snagging mountain.

Barns, sheds, and bunkhouses were downstream, along with the maze of corrals where the cattle could easily be moved about, doctored, branded, and separated according to age and sex. All set against the enormous backdrop of the Sawtooth mountains vaulting toward heaven.

The labor had been done by skilled construction men brought in from San Francisco. Materials had been hauled in from the Chicago-Seattle Railroad terminal. The architect and engineers had been properly housed as they built the headquarters before ever a Texas cow was brought in or a cowboy behind it.

41

Money, Clint thought when he saw the complex of buildings, big money.

Putting the bay in the corral closest to the bunkhouse, he hung his saddle and bridle in the tack shed, tossed an armful of hay out for the bay to nibble on, then moved toward the milled-lumber bunkhouse.

Most of the working hands were camped out in distant pastures with a chuckwagon and a bedroll wagon to see to their necessities as they rounded up loose cattle, graded them out, and herded the prime beeves to another pasture in anticipation of the drive over to Livingston and the cattle-car trip to Chicago.

In the bunkhouse, Cooky Thorp, a portly cowboy with a leg so sprung by a falling bronc he could never ride again, sorted pebbles and clods out of a stack of pink beans on the table while grizzled old shirtless Shorty Hudspeth kneaded witch hazel liniment into his arthritic right shoulder. Curly Beard, a clean-shaven, scrawny old man with a head bald as a turkey egg, leafed through a catalog of saddles, bridles, cinches, hackamores, and all the fancy accessories. Curly was too close to retiring to the liar's bench to be ordering more tack, but he liked to look at the drawings and cuss the new doodads.

In the corner bunk, Don Lyles, not much younger than the others, sat morosely, his el-

42

bows on his knees, his face in his hands, staring at the scarred pine floor.

They were all too old to ride with the roundup crew, Clint realized, and what lay ahead put the fear in them.

Cooky might hold on awhile because it didn't take much strength to boil beans, but the others could hardly throw a loop, buck a bronc, or dog a steer anymore. Once they were paid off, they'd drift into town, do odd jobs, and slowly starve to death.

They knew it deep down.

" 'Lo, boys," Clint said at the doorway, wondering where they'd put his little brother.

As they recognized his voice and looked up, he saw a series of almost identical emotions cross their lined faces.

A sharp awareness, then fear, then a set, poker face and a glance around at the others making sure they were all together.

"You heard about Lee, I reckon," Cooky said first. "I'm sure sorry about it."

The others mumbled and nodded.

"How'd it happen?" Clint asked softly.

They glanced at each other nervously, and Shorty said, "Badger must have told you."

"Told me the kid was carrying a saddle and got too close to the shootin' stand."

"That's the way it was." Curly nodded along with old Don Lyles.

"Was an accident plain to see," Cooky added, looking at the beans and nudging out a small clod of dirt.

"How many slugs hit him?" Clint asked, puzzled by the tension in the room. There was fear, maybe even deception, on the faces of men he'd worked with for years.

"I never saw anything," Don said. "I was cleanin' out the barn."

"They had a blanket over him," Shorty said, looking down at his boots.

"It happened awful fast. I don't think he suffered any," Cooky said.

"Badger took care of it right off, then the sheriff come out to make it official," Curly added, turning a page of the catalog without looking at it.

"I guess it'd only take one of them fifty-caliber seven-hundred-grain balls to make a sudden end to a man," Clint said. "Knock you head over heels, I expect."

"Likely. I didn't see nothin'," Don said, studying his boots.

"Hey, boys! I'm good old Clint, remember?" Clint said sharply, trying to put on a smile. "You don't have to tippytoe around me!"

"It's just . . . so . . . sad . . . ," Cooky replied hesitantly. "You was close."

"Yes, we was. He didn't have any last words

44

for me or nothin'?"

"Like you said, the power of the Big Fifty don't leave much breathin' time," Shorty Hudspeth croaked. "I wish I could go that quick."

"Well, tomorrow morning you can put your saddle on your shoulder and walk on over there in the killing park and bugle like an elk and let's see if you go as fast!" Clint said savagely, his voice ripping through their mumbles and murmurs.

"It's your job," Cooky said resentfully. "If you hadn't throwed yourself in jail, likely —"

"Likely what? Likely Lee would be settin' here, writin' your old yarns down?"

"I'm sayin' it's none of our fault." Cooky Thorp glared at Clint. "We're all just tryin' to do the best we can."

"Well, where is he?" Clint asked bluntly. "I reckon he ought to have a proper funeral."

In unison they all looked up and stared at him.

"What the hell is wrong?" Clint burst out, confused by the conflicting emotions swirling about his head.

"I guess Badger didn't tell you," Don said.

"We buried him this afternoon up on the knoll." Curly sighed.

"There was nobody to read over him, so

we all said a silent prayer," Shorty said softly. "It was the best we could do."

"Was the sheriff there?" Clint asked bitterly.

"He was here earlier. He didn't stay."

"Did the men who killed him come?" Clint asked bleakly. "Or was it just you four and Badger?"

Don looked at the floor again and nodded.

"I thank you for your kindness, boys," Clint said, "but what was the hellish hurry?"

"Badger . . . ," Curly Beard murmured.

"Badger wanted it all cleaned up and over with, pronto. Sure. That's old Badger, always managin' things," Clint growled, then turned and went back outside.

Darkness gathered in the hard-packed yard as Clint hurried toward the knoll that pushed up from the valley floor a quarter mile outside the ranch complex.

A swift-running, water-chiming creek skirted the far edge of the knoll and curved into the river, but it was shallow and there were plenty of stepping stones to cross on.

A game trail angled to the flattened top of the rise, and as the last of the light in the valley was swallowed up in darkness, Clint saw the mound of fresh earth.

There was no marker except a broken-handled shovel someone had left behind.

Clint knelt by the grave and put his hands into the fresh earth, wanting to groan out his grief and pain. But, shuddering, he took a deep breath, raised his head, and looked over the dark valley and the soft yellow light coming from the windows of the lodge.

The three owners with their three women would be having supper about now. They'd brought their chefs and servants as well as their bodyguards. They would be pouring the wine and eating roast buffalo hump or fresh-caught brook trout or duck breasts in orange marmalade.

Afterward they would smoke their cigars and discuss new ways of accumulating more wealth. Then they would go to their silk sheets and trained women.

They would not have bad dreams. They would not stir restlessly in their sleep. They would not even remember that they'd killed a boy that day.

Yet, it wasn't that way, he thought, shaking off his anger. The old cowboys were afraid. Why?

What did he know for sure? Only what had been told to him by quaking old men.

You must find out, he told himself. There's no other way.

Still on his knees, he took the broken shovel and commenced scooping the loose dirt from

47

the grave. It was hard, silent work, invisible to the world.

When the shovel caught on fabric, he set it aside, leaned down, and cupped the dirt out with his hands.

They'd not bothered to even build a box. They'd done just what Shorty said, wrapped him in a blanket and planted him quick.

With most of the earth removed, Clint leaned down into the grave, lighted a phosphor with his left hand and lifted back the gray blanket.

Keeping the phosphor low, he saw a bloody wound in the left hip that would have made a cripple for life out of any man but not necessarily killed him.

He moved the phosphor and saw another terrible wound in the right shoulder, a crippling but not lethal shot.

The phosphor burned his fingers and he struck another. This time holding it over the waxen face, the rigid lips, the closed eyes, he saw the third wound halfway between the blond eyebrows and the curly yellow hair.

He saw the singed eyebrows, scorched hair, and half-inch hole with black powder burned into the unlined and unblemished forehead of his brother. An execution.

# CHAPTER 3

*Something's not right, and it's big . . . You'd
make the best cattleman in Montana if you ever
decide to grow up . . .*

Clint looked off at the great mountains sil-
houetted against a pale white moon and vi-
sualized what must have happened. Somebody
had gotten Lee afoot and drove him like an
animal until a slug from a Big Fifty hit him
in the shoulder. Must have knocked him
down, but little brother was game and still
had two legs. Lee must have tried to run for
cover when the next slug smacked through
his hip, dropping him to flounder about, while
the third hunter strolled up, poked the big
barrel close to the kid's head, and pulled the
trigger. *Thump.* Then nothing except the sick
smell of burned meat and hair.

All three shots could have been fired by
one man, but likely the three hunters had
taken turns.

Sporting gents.

*After you, sir.* Boom! *Dash it all, he dodged.
Never mind, he's running slow now. May I
try, if you don't mind?* Boom!

49

*Good shot, dear fellow!*

*No, he's still alive.*

*Then I presume it's my turn for the coup de grâce.* Thump! *Stout fellow!*

Oh, you sonsabitches, Clint thought, I'll cut your fat hides into strips and feed 'em to the coyotes!

Calm down, he told himself. There's the top dogs and their three hired guns, and Badger's in on it and so's the sheriff. Even those old farts down in the bunkhouse are covering up. You make a wrong move, you'll be wolf bait before ever getting started.

Drawing the gray blanket back over the pale, luminescent face, Clint said aloud, "Don't worry, little brother. I'll get them. It's just goin' to take a while."

Probably the bodyguards drove Lee, herding him into the shooting stand. Trying to veer off, there'd always be a plug-ugly heading him with a gun, keeping him moving toward the killing ground. Probably couldn't believe it. Probably thought he'd be all right once he found the three bosses, who'd tell their hired guns to quit playing games. Then that massive shock in the shoulder.

Lee must have known then, all right. Maybe he couldn't comprehend that anyone could be so cold-blooded, but he'd known with that first startling hit that there were men in the world who would hunt down another man without thought of punishment. He'd known that he'd underestimated the savagery of gentlemen.

No telling how much time it had taken to flush him out again and deliver the shattering hip wound. The mercy shot would have come in the time it took for the gent to stroll over a hundred yards, lay the .50-caliber muzzle on that fair brow, the blue eyes beneath still blazing, then *thump,* the head bouncing off the ground with only death's shudder left in the slack form.

That's why they wrapped him in the blanket and planted him so fast. Once it was done, there was no quick way of hiding the truth of that final shot. *No way to explain it, so cover it up and who'll question our word?*

*Who even cares? His brother's a fiddle-footed joker, doesn't know beans from buckshot. Fool him easy enough. And even if he figures it out, still, what can he do to the most powerful men in Montana, maybe in the whole country?*

They probably expected Clint to shed a few tears and then play the fool the way he always had. If he looked a little bronco, well, they'd have themselves another drive. Wouldn't that be good sport!

A mad, eerie grin split Clint's lean hounddog face. Oh, yes, you sonsabitches, the clown

51

can read your tracks.

Slowly pushing the loose dirt back into the grave, Clint let his thoughts roam. A pattern formed, ideas for action merged to sketch a strategy for survival until he could settle the score.

Simple enough to catch the three of them together and burn them down with a six-gun, then hope to get clear of the bodyguards.

He remembered what Lee had wanted: ". . . suppose all three had to stand public trial before a jury of their peers. . . ."

Lee couldn't have known the charge would be his own murder, but bringing the three to justice would be the most fitting way to avenge Lee's death.

It would mean gathering evidence.

They would end their dealings in a few days, a week at the most. That might make it harder, but it would be done.

He wished now he'd paid some attention to them, but he had been too busy playing the fool to care about which one got up early or which one took an evening stroll, or which one had a weak spot and which one didn't.

Well, you'll have to learn, clown.

By the light of the moon, he carried slabs of hard shale from the side of the knoll and crisscrossed them three high over the grave so that no animal could dig down and disturb the bones of his only brother.

Satisfied with the sanctity of the grave, Clint looked down at the lamplight in the windows and heard an accordion playing the "Varsuvienne."

They're dancing! he thought, astonished. They kill my brother for sport in the morning and go dancing in the night!

Learn, clown, learn that they're merciless, without conscience or decency. Three tycoons, three sparkling doxies, and three strong-arm men expert with club, knife, and gun.

Evidence. A jury trial. A public hanging.

His thoughts returned more calmly to the rock-slabbed grave and what his smiling golden-haired brother had meant to him and what they had meant to each other. One steady, on his way to being a top journalist in his time. The other a damfool cowboy joker, always going downhill the easiest way possible.

Bowing his head, his eyes filled, he said huskily, "We come to a fork in the trail. You got to go your way and me mine. I just hope we meet up again and ride awhile together. . . . Lee . . . little brother . . . So long."

Leaving the dark knoll, Clint made his way down the trail in the cold moonlight, stopped at a water trough, and scrubbed his face. He then made his way back to the bunkhouse.

Cooky had finished sorting the beans and was playing checkers with Shorty Hudspeth, while Curly Beard and Don Lyles sat on their bunks, watching.

Once again, Clint felt the room freeze. They were all afraid he'd done just what they feared most.

A rigidity and a watchfulness. Maybe they'd seized up in the hinges after so many years cowboyin', but their wits were all the more cunning in the world of endurance.

Someone had warned them: Be quiet or you'll have no home, come winter.

For a second he felt sorry for them and wondered if he ever got old, would he too sell out his pride and independence for board and room?

No one dared ask where he'd been and he broke the strained silence by saying, "I been rockin' up Lee's grave. Keep the varmints out."

They relaxed some, believing him, and he added, "Right pretty lookout up there. You planted him so he can see what's goin' on all the time. I can give him a wave and howdy-do first thing in the mornings. I appreciate that, boys."

"We figured nobody cared about the knoll and it was as good a place as any," Curly said from his bunk.

"I suppose somebody collected his belongings?" Clint asked easy-like.

"Badger filled up a war bag with his goods," Cooky said. "It's over there on his bunk."

Clint went to the bunk next to Don's and dumped the canvas bag out on the mattress. "Not much for twenty years of livin'," Clint said, looking at the spare clothes, a brass belt buckle, razor, comb, bone-handled jackknife. Four dollars and some change. Six-gun in its gunbelt, rolled up. A can of peaches, a set of old iron spurs with pieces of a twenty-dollar gold piece sweated on the shanks that Lee had given a dollar for to a down-and-outer. A bottle of ink and a brass-nibbed pen, but no notebook to write in.

"I suppose his saddle is outside?" Clint asked.

"Never found his saddle," Shorty said, moving a checker.

"Nor his horse, for that matter," Curly said softly.

"I thought somebody said he was carryin' his saddle," Clint murmured, stowing the bag.

"Nobody said anything like that to us," Shorty said irritably.

"Hold it down, Shorty," Cooky said quickly. "Maybe it's outside on the railing or maybe it's still on the horse."

"Likely it'll turn up," Clint said noncommittally. "Or maybe you cowboys buried it with him and forgot about it."

"What the hell!" Shorty snorted nervously.

"We wouldn't forget," Curly said.

"I guess you're jokin', Clint," Cooky smiled. "You never was one for melancholy ways."

"We had some good times when he'd get you old veterans to talkin' and he'd start writin' your old lies down." Clint smiled.

"Too bad," Curly said, shaking his head sadly. "We all goin' to be dead plenty soon and now all them fine tales goin' to be dead with us."

"I ain't dyin' that soon," Don Lyles protested weakly. "Long as I can set a horse, I'll be all right."

"Sure, Don." Clint chuckled. "But the last time I saw you climb into a saddle, Lee was givin' you a boost up."

"That was a cold mornin'," Lyles retorted. "Anybody's stiffened up on a cold mornin'."

"I loaned that saddle to Lee. Had silver conchas all over it, remember?" Clint asked. "I give a Mexican saddlemaker a month's pay to make that saddle dazzle the señoritas . . ."

"It'll turn up just like a bad penny," Cooky said resignedly.

"You seem to be talkin' around somethin'," Curly said carefully. "Like you wasn't satisfied in your mind."

"Me? Old Panamint Clint? Sho now, you want to hear my new song?

> Susan Van Dusan
> Dyin' won't be gruesome
> If I know I'm past losin'
> My screw . . ."

No one laughed or even smiled.

"Want some more?" Clint asked, his old sprightly self again. "Another verse?"

"Not now," Cooky said grimly.

"I can't do it," Don Lyles moaned and hurried out the door into the night.

"What's got into old Don?" Clint asked in wonder. "Was it that bad a joke?"

"Clint, you was born a fool and can't change, I guess," Curly said disgustedly.

"Heck, Curly," Clint protested, "the kid's dead. Sure he was a good friend to all you rannies, but that's over with!"

"What's the matter with Don?" Badger's voice from the doorway caught them by surprise.

"He don't favor my new Susan Van Dusan verse." Clint laughed and turned to face the stocky foreman, who was entering the door, followed by pale Don Lyles.

"You're soundin' mighty cheerful for a time like this," Badger Corbin said evenly.

"I was just sayin' that Lee's up there in heaven cavortin' around like a fat pony in a field of oats, so there ain't no reason to be treadin' on your lower lip."

Gray-haired, weather-worn Badger Corbin stared at the tall, rangy cowboy, his deep-set eyes alert and keen, his face unreadable. After a moment, he shook his head and said, "You was always a joker — why change?"

"He was askin' about Lee's saddle," Cooky muttered, staring at the checkerboard.

"What about Lee's saddle?" Badger's head jerked up.

"I was just wonderin' where it is, seein' as how it was made special for me, anyways. I got more poontang with that saddle than you can ever imagine. Why, one time, down in Juarez —"

"There was a mix-up," Badger interrupted gruffly. "Likely the horse strayed over into the Crow Reservation."

"Then some lucky buck is getting a lot of squaw poontang with it right now." Clint laughed.

"I got to line out tomorrow's work," Badger growled. "Curly, you and Lyles check out the remuda in the south pasture."

"That's easy enough."

"Shorty, you think you can muck out the stables up at the lodge?"

"Reckon I can," Shorty said dully.

"I don't know why I keep you old carcasses on. You sure ain't good for anything," Badger growled, surveying the old men.

"They're loyal," Clint said.

"What do you mean by that?" Badger snapped.

"We're always loyal to the brand, just like other old cow outfits. We've rode day and night in rain or snow to make the cattle increase. Risked our necks a couple times a day for the brand. That's the way we are."

"I get your point. And now you can drive game for the hunters."

"That sounds real interestin'." Clint grinned.

"Take a wagon with their provisions and follow the surrey. The duke's valet can drive that."

"And them other two valets?" Clint asked.

"They ride with you. Better lead your horse."

"But—" Clint started to object.

"No buts," Badger snarled. "You don't like it, I'll write out your time."

"I like it! Don't be in such a hurry to get rid of good old funnyface Panamint Clint!" Clint laughed. "I was just thinkin' one of them valets could drive the wagon, and I could ride my bay."

59

"Do it my way, Durby," Badger growled. "And don't play no jokes on those dudes. They ain't got any sense of humor."

"I'm loyal, boss." Clint grinned and glanced around at the older punchers.

Badger stared at him again, his eyes suspicious, doubting, yet undecided. "I'll sure be glad when the crew gets back from the gather," he growled. "Maybe somethin' will start makin' sense."

"You boys want me to tell you a bedtime story before I tuck you in?" Clint yawned, sitting on the edge of his bunk, prying off his boots.

"That's the only smart thing you've said all night," Cooky said. "Bunk time."

In a few minutes the lamps were blown out and the men commenced their individual night noises, snoring in different keys, making tremulous whistles and small complaining groans.

Clint stared into the darkness. He felt like he'd passed by tiredness and could go for days and nights without sleep. . . .

They'd lied about the saddle when they cooked up the story about Lee looking like an elk. None of them would mention the notebook, even though it was the most obvious thing missing from Lee's effects.

And they were in it together. Maybe directly in on Lee's murder or just keeping quiet about it, but now they all had to hang together and hope Clint Durby would just get bored and drift along.

Sleep caught him from behind when he didn't expect it, and he never knew it until he heard Cooky's yell.

"Wake, snakes, day's abreakin'!"

He listened to their groaning as they pushed their arthritic joints into painful action. Not waiting for them, Clint dressed, buckled on his worn six-gun, went outside and washed his face, then made his way to the cookhouse. Cooky was pouring coffee with one hand and turning flapjacks with the other.

"Mornin', world," Clint sang out into the grouchy complaints. "Let's make it a good one!"

"Oh, shut up, for Christ's sake," Badger growled, burning his lip on the enameled tin cup.

They ate in silence and went their different ways. Clint finished his breakfast, dumped his dirty dishes in a boiler half full of soapy water, and went over to the corral, where he found the four heavy workhorses so tame he didn't need to rope them. They accepted their halters and he led them over to the spring wagon, where he harnessed them on either side of the wagon tongue.

"How are you at herdin' jackrabbits?" he

asked the bay as he tied his lead rope to the rear of the wagon.

Climbing to the wagon seat, he glanced up yonder at the knoll, nodded his head, and thought, smiling, Mornin', little brother, maybe today we can make a stab at findin' justice.

Pulling up at the rear of the lodge, cooks and servants swarmed out with hampers of food and beverages, silver, porcelain, and crystal, blankets, sunshades, and a portable table and chairs.

Loaded up, he drove the wagon around to the front of the great log building and saw the surrey waiting at the front steps.

Pulling up behind, Clint noticed that the driver was the middle-sized man known as Tony Douglas, the Duke of Dorset's valet. He looked as if he might be a grocer or liveryman until you saw the thin scars beetling his eyebrows, the flat nose, the cabbaged ears, and the wary look in his eye that meant he was more than ready all the time.

On his left ring finger he wore a large, gold-plated ring with a glass diamond suitable for chopping a man's face into raw meat.

Coming down the broad stairway were the empire builders themselves, togged out in tailored outdoorsman's wear.

Leading the group, Clint recognized Big Jim

Ralston, king of the Chicago-Seattle Railroad. His broad belly bobbed as he came down the steps, but more important was the short neck that pedestaled a head of equal width. The line from the collarbone up to the ear bulged out a little on either side. His head was a great scowling chunk of oak. His mustache curved around to meet his sideburns, and the heavy eyebrows looked like black caterpillars. A glance from those deep-set eyes made a cinder of Clint and passed on, seeking more fuel to torch.

A step behind and to the right of Ralston came Senator Lorenzo Cooley, a man so short he would have been called a dwarf had he not tried to reach the sky with his straight back and neck as he trotted down the steps. He too was well fed, but the paunch was higher up, as if it belonged to his protruding chest. Clint thought that for all the world he looked just like a robin redbreast.

A step behind and to the left came an elongated man, tall and stooped, with a craggy, horse face, a benevolent-uncle type until you saw the sour set of his mouth and the quick-shifting eyes.

Following the tall Englishman came a man so huge he hadn't ever found a ready-made suit to fit his bulk. Like Tony Douglas, Mike Mikowski had the marks of a bruiser on his face, but he'd not got them in street fights or the squared circle. He'd come up through the ranks of railroad builders to gang boss, and he could drive men to lay more steel than any other gang and no one dared offer a complaint or pause for rest.

The other man, Red McLaglen, was a match for size. A redhead with broad shoulders, girth, and long, powerful legs, his sledge-hammer jaw jutted out farther than his flat nose, and there was a look of humor on his reddish, freckled countenance that was absent from Mikowski's. The senator had found him in his home state of Pennsylvania puddling iron for a dollar a day.

Without pausing, Big Jim Ralston heaved his bulk into the surrey's backseat and settled down like a giant toad, waiting for the others.

The senator took the front seat by Tony Douglas, and the tall Englishman walked around and climbed up to the seat next to the Railroad King.

Appearing on the front veranda of the lodge, three ladies dressed in odd costume for cattle country came to the peeled-pine railing and cried out feminine shrieks of farewell.

One dark-haired girl was dressed in a soft green dress with a red jacket and what might pass as a conical Robin Hood hat made of green felt.

The young woman next to her wore a gown of light material like gauze that floated in the breeze when she waved her arm, and the third wore a pale blue dress with contrasting ruffles and a striped silk sacque above it.

Clint wondered whose was whose, and decided it wasn't important. They all had hourglass figures and pallid complexions. They all were dressed expensively and extravagantly.

The dark-haired Robin Hood seemed to be distinguishable from the others by a seriousness in her eyes and a liveliness different from the languor of the other two.

When Mikowski and McLaglen climbed up to the spring seat beside him, Clint slid over as far as he could to make room for their broad butts.

"Mornin', gents," Clint said. "How's your health and corporosity?"

"Can you drive this team?" McLaglen growled.

"I reckon," Clint piped up cheerily. "If they've got the strength to pull us."

"Keep up with the surrey," Mikowski said with a trace of an accent in his gravelly voice, "and you'll be all right."

# CHAPTER 4

Where were these thugs when Lee was gunned down? Clint wondered as the team patiently followed in the surrey's dust. They had to have been close by. And why hadn't they simply been assigned the dirty job, leaving the bosses out of it?

"What are they goin' to shoot today?" Clint asked, making conversation.

"It don't make much difference to them, just so it bleeds," McLaglen said.

"Game's gettin' scarce. Less every day," Mikowski grumbled.

"You can't find any better huntin' any-where," Clint said idly.

"But after a few days, the creatures begin to get the idea," McLaglen chuckled deep in his chest, "and they go visit their rela-tives."

The surrey took the right fork of the trace and kept to its left the monumental white and pink cliff with its cascading hot mineral water, aiming up a side valley that by itself could have held two prosperous cattle ranches. On either side of the great pasture were timbered

66

hills rolling toward the hard thrust of the Saw-tooths.

A pretty little stream meandered down through the valley, and the wagon trace forded it once, then stayed on the south side. Clint estimated there were a thousand Texas long-horns in the side valley, but the range was so big, they seemed scarce. Along the slopes near the timber he saw a herd of young elk and another of big deer, and far up the valley the flashing tails of antelope. There would be some moose in the lowland brakes along the creek, and a small herd of buffalo ran toward the mountains as they approached. There would be timber wolves and bears in equal abundance.

"Big country," Clint said with wonder at the huge, primitive richness.

"There must be half a dozen other feeder valleys that would hold more shooting stands," McLaglen said, nodding wisely.

"But you'll only be here a few more days," Clint said.

"Sure, but how about their friends? Charge 'em a fortune to come out and shoot a buffalo. Hell, they'd coin the money."

"I guess they got so much already . . . ," Mikowski muttered.

"I wish they'd give me just half of this one valley," Clint said.

"Keep on wishing. One thing I've learned

about the rich is they never give nothing away." McLaglen chuckled again.

"That's right," Mikowski nodded. "Somehow it's always the other way."

"I guess it's like the feller who took so much medicine he was sick a long time after he got well." Clint laughed, stretching his mouth down and screwing up his mobile features to look like a very sick man.

The burly men looked at him curiously and didn't laugh.

"You're that clown we heard about," McLaglen said, nodding.

"Just say I like a good time," Clint said cheerfully.

"Your brother —"

"Like the soldiers say, hurrah for the next one of us to go!" Clint chuckled.

"I don't get it," Mikowski growled.

"Oh, there's always a nut on every family tree." Clint laughed again.

Mikowski relaxed and grinned. "And you're it, eh?"

The surrey came to a natural park near the stream where rough benches and tables were set up, as well as a firepit with a blackened iron grill.

"All the comforts of home," Clint said, halting the team and climbing down to the soft, springy ground.

Great ponderosa pines lifted their heads into the big sky, and breezes played through their needled limbs like heavenly harps.

Off to the side a pole had been lashed between two pines for hanging smaller game, and next to it was a blood-stained sled for bringing in the elk and buffalo carcasses.

A hundred yards upstream, Clint saw the three separate wooden platforms screened with pine boughs; they were spaced far enough apart that the shooters could pick their own shots, but close enough that they could call out to each other. The stands overlooked a long open meadow rutted with ancient game trails.

As the servants unloaded the wagon, Clint ambled to the nearest elevated stand, went up the three steps, and saw a comfortable camp chair close to the edge where the cross railing could be used as a rest for the Big Fifty.

Surveying the scene, he thought, this is where they said they did it. There didn't seem to be any kind of cover in the grassy park, but they'd said the kid had come through brushy timber with his saddle on his shoulder.

"Looking for something?"

The voice was cold and crisp, and the words pronounced in a way Clint had never heard before.

Turning to face the tall, craggy Englishman,

Clint smiled and said, "Mornin', Duke, I was just lookin' over the killin' ground."

Eagle eyes tried to pierce through his smiling mask, but Clint's will was the stronger, and the English aristocrat blinked and said, "Fetch my rifle and after this you may address me as 'Your Lordship.'"

"Yes, sir." Clint grinned and nodded. "Won't be a minute, Your Lordship."

"Oaf," the duke snarled at Clint's back and settled himself in the camp chair, drew out a burlwood pipe, and stuffed it leisurely with a fragrant tobacco mixture. He waited until the middleweight, Tony Douglas, sprang forward, striking a phosphor as he came, so that as the duke settled back in the chair, the flame hovered over the pipe bowl.

The duke waited until the phosphor was close to burning Tony's fingers before dragging the fire down into the pipe. It was an ancient ritual between them, and Tony Douglas prided himself on the simple fact that he never flinched from the flame.

"Who's the beater?" the duke asked idly.

"I never got his name yet, Your Lordship," Tony said in his bouncy Cockney accent.

"See that you do. Surly sort, likely a blackguard," the duke said.

When Clint returned with the heavy rifle cased in a buckskin scabbard, the middleweight watchdog eyed him closely, taking the rifle at the top of the steps and barring Clint from coming further.

"You —" Tony Douglas said, "you have a name?"

"Call me Clint." Clint grinned. "I'm the only one of my friends I can count on."

The Cockney didn't smile. "Watch your step, mate. We don't need no jokers."

"They say, 'Smile and the world smiles with you.' " Clint chuckled and rolled his eyes.

"I have him now, Tony," the duke said languidly over his shoulder. "He's the jester brother of the poor lad who appeared to be an elk."

Tony Douglas flushed, feeling that he'd somehow failed in his duty. His left shoulder rose as he shifted his feet and balled his knobby fists. "No more the merry-andrew with me, cowboy, or I'll cut you to pieces. Clear out of here."

"Shucks," Clint mumbled, backing away apologetically. "Don't be mad just because I'm a poor ignorant country boy."

Douglas tucked his chin behind his left shoulder and suddenly shot out a left jab that barely touched Clint's chin but still had enough force to snap his head back.

"That's a taste." Douglas smiled crookedly. "There's more if you want it."

Clint backed clear, protesting weakly, "Not me, I'm peaceable . . ."

Once clear, he walked back to the wagon, passing the ponderous Big Jim Ralston and the short senator.

He noticed that Ralston's ferocious glare was chronic; the man appeared to be all set to lunge forward like a crazed bull and wreak havoc on whatever was nearest.

The senator took this massive threat in stride, a sly twinkle in his eye as he held his own popinjay dignity against the mountainous financier.

Again Clint felt roasted by the raging eyes of the big man and thought he could see the senator make a check mark in the back of his head without ever altering his expression: Watch this cowboy.

Then Clint smiled at himself for thinking he was that important to the senator's world.

". . . All it will take is a barrel of whiskey and a free ride to Washington," Big Jim was saying as they passed by.

"We've always got the Army . . . ," the senator replied.

Clint made his way through the bodyguards and servants setting up the big harvest table, which was now covered by a gleaming damask cloth. He smelled oak burning in the firepit, and saw green bottles of champagne chilling in a wickerwork basket in an eddy of the icy stream.

Clint thought back to the time in Kansas when their mama had taken him and Lee to a restaurant, figuring to educate them in the world's fancy ways, and they'd both ordered the best thing they could think of: crackers and milk.

A bellow from behind broke into his memory: "You there, beater!"

Clint turned to face Ralston and nodded. "Yessir?"

"We'll want elk today," Ralston growled.

"Shucks, I thought you'd want a batch of grizzly bears." Clint smiled.

Sudden silence. The busy activity of the servants ceased as they froze, mouths open in shock.

"That's enough!" Ralston snarled furiously, taking a step forward. "You ever talk back to me again, you'll regret it."

Ralston stood like a volcano ready to explode.

Clint held his gaze and said, "Elk."

"Big ones. I want their eyeteeth for big men in high places," Ralston growled.

"Big eyeteeth," Clint said straight-faced.

"Fool!" The burly man turned on his heel and strode off toward the shooting stands.

It couldn't have been here, Clint thought,

watching the bulky railroad king's wide back, bull neck, and blunt head. Too many servants. You couldn't keep this many people quiet about the murder. It was somewhere else.

It was somewhere they could drive the surrey to, a rendezvous close to this valley.

Clint saw Badger Corbin ride up and go immediately to the big man. His speech hit Badger like lightning bolts, judging by the way he looked over at Clint.

Obviously it was a command to get rid of Clint, put him to work, or cut out his tongue.

Untying the bay from the back of the wagon, Clint slipped the bit into his mouth and the crown strap back over its ears.

I guess you grow up by being treated like a dog, he thought, running his hand down the bay's gleaming neck fondly, waiting for another dressing-down.

It didn't take long. Badger Corbin rode close, jerked his sorrel to a halt, and snapped, "You and your big mouth!"

"I hope you explained that I'm just a fool joker at heart," Clint said.

"They'da fired us both except I told 'em you was the brother to Lee," Badger said grimly. "It seems they took pity on you."

"They should," Clint muttered. "A poor old half-wit like me havin' to make a livin' in this hard world . . ."

"I never knew you to downgrade yourself before," Badger said suspiciously.

"I'm just tryin' to grow up . . . Besides, I still owe Lee's fancy college a hundred dollars. I'm also tryin' to figure how to tell if an elk has big eyeteeth. Guess I'll have to lasso him, bust him down to the ground, and pry his jaw open to see."

"Big elk have big teeth," Corbin snapped.

"No offense, Badger, but the big elk won't be down off the mountain for another month."

Badger stared at him, knowing he was right. "We've got to give 'em somethin'," he said, shaking his head.

"Maybe there's a few young ones around." Clint tightened the rimfire rig, and mounted in one swift motion. "Maybe they won't know the difference."

"Hold on," Badger said, coming alongside Clint, "we're to move 'em east to west. Just spook 'em along slow and easy, then come up hard and hootin' when we're close, and hope to hell they'll run in the right direction."

"Shucks, I thought it might be a hard thing to do." Clint smiled and winked. "What's say we just get it over with and be home by dinnertime?"

Badger stared angrily at the tall cowboy, then wheeled his sorrel and spurred him into a gallop toward the upper end of the valley.

Using his knees, Clint got the same speed out of the bay and was alongside Badger as he crossed the shallow stream and aimed diagonally for the other side.

Clint pointed off to his left where, near the timber, a couple of young bull elk and a few cows and calves were feeding.

Bringing the sorrel down to a trot, Badger rasped, "We'll circle around back. Just hearin' the horses ought to move 'em westerly."

"We'll lose 'em if they run," Clint said. "Best just graze 'em along like you said till we're close to the sportsmen, then ki-yi 'em on across."

Clint guided the bay uphill through the big pines until he judged he could turn an elk trying to break around, then head him due east toward the shooting stand.

Walking the bay slowly, he reckoned the elk would hear the little noise from his hoof falls and amble on east just to stay clear.

It was no way to hunt, he thought, but the rich men only wanted the eyeteeth, the bigger the better.

Anybody in his right mind wouldn't hunt elk before the first frost, when the old ones would come down off the mountains, big and fat and when you killed one it would be so cold the meat wouldn't spoil.

Off to his right he glimpsed a spiral of buzzards through the trees, but before he could pin down a landmark beneath it, the trees closed in again and he was left to wonder what was so interesting on over the rise.

Feeling they were getting close to the hunters, he eased the bay downhill to where he could see the terrain better, then realized they would be crossing a low, grassy swale where the elk might turn back toward him.

Quietly he eased the bay back to bar the way. Halting in the grassy bottom of virgin pasture he saw the fresh tracks of a shod horse and wheel tracks.

Couldn't be older than a couple of days, for no pine needles had drifted into the prints and the bent grass hadn't returned to its natural condition.

He waited a minute, and not hearing any elk breaking up his way, he turned the bay down toward the edge of the timber where he saw Badger Corbin sitting on his halted horse, head turned his way.

Seeing Clint, he lifted his hat high, then spurred the sorrel forward and gave a howling, "Yow-eeee!"

Clint whirled the bay and set him galloping across the slope, ki-yi-ing for all his might, until he saw the brown and orange elk fleeing ahead of him in great leaps. As they started to break away uphill, he waved his hat and howled like a hungry wolf, and the elk turned back, running hard.

The elk charged pell-mell across the killing ground, and Clint pulled up the bay while the Big Fifties thundered from their screened stands.

The two leaders made it across and into the timber without a scratch, and the cows were almost across when a wild bullet dropped a squalling calf. Its mother faltered and another bullet broke her shoulder.

A long silence hovered over the meadow as the cow tried to push along on her hind legs, and after a while a tall, stoop-shouldered figure walked across the meadow to the wounded elk, placed the muzzle against the head, and fired. *Thump*. The cow collapsed, and the Englishman strolled back toward the shooting stand.

The mercy shot. Sportsman to the core, Clint thought, kneeing the bay toward camp, but staying close to the trees. If anyone mistook him for an elk, he wanted some cover nearby.

As Badger and Clint rode up to the wagon and dismounted, they were met by the three sportsmen. Their anger was apparent before a word was spoken.

"Too small and too fast — and not an eyetooth to show!" Big Jim Ralston had the first say. "You're worthless."

"You should know what is required," Senator Cooley threatened. "If you're too stupid to learn, we'll find somebody else who damn well can."

"Mindless herders, screaming at game. Imagine!" the duke said with a contemptuous smile. "You ought to be mucking out stables."

"They're wild —" Badger tried to explain. "They wouldn't have come across that open meadow less'n we'd scared the pie-waddin' out of 'em."

"In England, it's quite simple. Of course, our game managers have a spot of intelligence," the duke said disdainfully. Turning to the senator and Ralston, he added, "I vote to fire the bloody lot of them."

"Later . . . ," the senator said. "After our . . . arrangement."

Ralston glowered at the senator and the duke, paused a moment, then growled, "Not yet."

"Thank you kindly. We'll try to do better," Badger said apologetically, taking off his hat and looking at the ground.

"The day's ruined," the duke said, his gaze resting on Clint, who was trying to look repentant. "I suggest we return to the lodge for proper accommodations."

The senator said, "We've got to work

through a lot of details before Friday, and I need that memo of understanding . . ."

"We're going," Ralston growled as he hoisted himself into the surrey.

"What about that meat out in the meadow?" Badger croaked.

"Reserve the loins for our table, leave the rest," the senator said, and took the front seat again.

After a moment the tall English aristocrat took his place in the back beside the massive Ralston, and the surrey moved out.

The cow and calf were butchered by the chef and his helper, the choice backstraps wrapped in clean cloths and loaded into the wagon box, while Clint held the team, nervous from the smell of fresh blood, under control.

"There'd be more room for you if I rode my horse," Clint said to Mikowski. "The team will head straight for home."

"Fine with me," Mikowski said. "They get smart with me, I'll break their goddamned necks."

Looking back, Clint saw black specks in the western sky, and as the caravan started back down the trace toward ranch headquarters, he held the bay back, then pulled him up and dismounted as the servants' wagon passed by.

"Need any help?" the pasty-faced cook called out.

80

"Picked up a stone —" Clint shook his head. "I'll be along after a while."

When the wagon was gone, Clint mounted the bay and quickly turned back up the valley. Putting the bay into a full gallop, he arrived at the mouth of the grassy swale before the gelding started blowing hard.

As he guided the long-legged bay up the feeder valley, watching the tracks of the shod horse, the wagon-wheel marks close by, and the occasional prints of low-heeled shoes, Clint saw the buzzards circling nearly overhead.

Rounding a bend, he entered a small clearing where the stench of decay turned his stomach.

Buzzards soared away as he approached the bloated horse, its legs poked stiffly skyward. The gas-filled belly curled over the restraining cinch, and somewhere underneath was a saddle with Mexican silver conchas decorating its fenders.

He recognized the bridle as one he'd made himself and loaned the kid. Empty eye sockets stared through the leather frame. The buzzards knew where to start first. Just behind the head, the spine had been blown out.

He stepped upwind of the dead horse and looked about the clearing.

Why had Lee been riding up this little lonesome valley?

There was no reason. He couldn't possibly drive game from it.

So he'd been sent on an errand. Likely he'd made some kind of a drive about as foolish as the one they'd just finished, rode into camp, and someone, probably Badger Corbin, had told him to go up the swale and check the country out. . . .

Ranging afoot up the little valley, he found where the wheel tracks stopped, the grass crushed by men's boots.

So they'd come up ahead of Lee. They'd been waiting.

Crisscrossing the head of the valley, Clint found three separate ambuscades where they'd waited for the kid.

First, down his horse and put him afoot. Then wing him and you've got your man.

From the elevation of the sharpshooter, he could see how Lee had cleared the horse as it fell. A few steps away, the shoulder shot must have knocked him down.

Only a single lightning-blasted bull pine made any cover.

Say he made it to the pine, then what? He couldn't return the fire with his short-range six-gun and a broken right shoulder.

So he'd had to make a run across open ground to the nearest timber. Somewhere between that blasted pine and the timber, he'd taken the ball in the hip, and there he'd waited.

Clint walked slowly back down to the flat, and a few feet away from the dead horse, he saw the black stain on the green grass, with ants working at it. The ground was scored by a pair of hard-running boot heels that led over to the bull pine; there, blood clotted on the ground where the wounded young man had assessed his chances.

With bleak eyes Clint followed the boot trail halfway to the timber, where he saw the broad blood spill caked on the grass and covered with ants.

Here the blasted hip had stopped him. Here he gazed up at the killers as they approached, unable to believe what he was seeing. "Hey, gents, what's the idea?"

No, he knew well enough, and he'd looked up with only the desperate hope that the Cavalry might come over the hill or his big brother come riding around the bend with a six-shooter blazing in each hand.

He'd seen the black muzzle of the big rifle rise up slowly and it had looked as big as a cave.

*Thump.* The sound of a yellow-haired head smacking the ground.

The huge .50-170-700 cartridge case lay gleaming in the grass.

He tucked it into his shirt pocket and retraced the route, searching. The notebook had to be somewhere. There were no saddle-bags on the dead horse. It hadn't been in his war bag.

Crouching at the base of the dead trunk as Lee must have done, Clint saw the curl of the ripped bark, tugged at the upper edge of it, then, giving a hard yank, broke the thick bark pocket loose in his hands. Ants scrambled for safety from their exposed workings.

Nothing but ants.

Clint's heart sank.

The killers already had the notebook. They'd only needed to silence the writer.

# CHAPTER 5

Plain-out murder, he thought, riding the bay down the wagon trace toward the lodge. The three of them had figured out the crossfire trap, and told Badger to send young Lee Durby up the canyon. Once started, the hired hooligans had followed on foot, keeping him moving into the hunters' trap.

Hardly call it hunting. More like standing in a slaughter pen knocking steers down with an eight-pound hammer.

The law hadn't troubled them. Never had.

Later they'd hauled Lee's body down to the shooting stand, told Badger it was an accident and to fix it up with the sheriff.

Maybe money had passed hands. Maybe it was just the unspoken promise that not only Badger but Sheriff Cox would always have a job so long as nobody rocked the boat.

Then somebody made a mistake. Somebody couldn't just say Lee had been shot accidentally. Somebody had to build up the story so it seemed believable; had to say he was carrying his saddle high on his shoulder in the brush, so he looked like an elk, not knowing

I prized that silver-mounted saddle some and might wonder where it went to.

And now there's only the fool clown lookin' for justice.

Six . . . seven . . . eight of them are in it, and that's a pretty fair-sized job for one joker.

No help from the hands. They know there's something haywire, but they don't want to ride the grubline next winter. They call it bein' loyal to the brand.

Cowboy knows he's responsible for the cows and he'll ride day and night because it's a matter of honor for him, something he was taught from the time he could set a saddle. He can't unlearn it except by turnin' into an outlaw or worse. His loyalty to the brand is the same as his own self-respect.

So bein' loyal to the brand means loyal to the owner, and if the Syndicate says to hush up, the old hands hush up. Maybe they don't like it, but their rheumatism tells 'em it's loyalty to the brand.

After unsaddling and turning out the bay, Clint walked toward the bunkhouse, singing in an off-key falsetto:

"O Susan Van Dusan
We'll sure make a twosome
Or maybe a threesome
Dependin' on you . . ."

The old hands stared at him in the doorway, worry in their rheumy eyes, trembling in their splayed and knotted fingers.

"Where you been?" Badger Corbin slouched out of the shadows, his eyes boring into Clint's.

"The bay picked up a stone and bruised his foot," Clint replied easily. "I been collectin' blisters on my extremities just walkin' home."

"You rode in all right."

"The last mile." Clint nodded. "I'll be damned if I'm goin' to show myself afoot leadin' a fool horse."

"I could believe it or not believe it," Badger growled, not letting up.

"Hell, Badger, you never asked for an accountin' when we got caught in the norther and I rode out eight horses in twenty-four hours," Clint replied hotly. "I reckon you smelt around the wrong hound-dog's butt this time. Just write up my time. I'm sick of all you gloomy pallbearers anyways."

"Hold steady," Badger said, his eyes shifting. "The bosses figure I ought to know where the hands are all the time, but I don't aim to lose a top hand over it."

"Top hand? Me! Clint the clown?" Clint laughed. "I'll be damned. I never thought anybody ever noticed."

"Don't let it make you any dizzier than you are," Cooky broke in.

"We're ridin' out early," Badger said. "Bosses goin' to the telegraph office first thing, but us poor cowboys are goin' to comb the north slopes for strays."

"Shucks, I was hopin' we'd go huntin' again," Clint grumbled.

Midsummer daybreak came not very long after midsummer sunset in the north country, and Clint groaned with the others when he heard Cooky's wake-up call.

After a sturdy breakfast, Clint rode his short-coupled gray through his morning crow-hops, a ritual of protest, then the gray settled down and hung his head as they waited for the other riders to get their rickety fingers loosened up to rope their mounts, fumble with cinch leathers, and set their bridles.

The old-timers cussed when they missed a throw they could have made blindfolded ten years earlier, and grumbled when the lifting of a saddle sent sharp pains into their elbows and shoulders.

Clint appeared to be half asleep, but he was turned to have a sidewise view of the lodge, where he saw the six-passenger Rockaway coach standing at the front entrance with a four-horse team in the traces and the Cockney middleweight holding down the driver's seat.

Three bosses off to start some dirty work, and three mistresses to stroll the boardwalk of Sawtooth and pretend to be shopping. There wasn't a damned thing in Sawtooth they'd want. Even the best meal they could get at Ike's Cafe couldn't compare to the feasts at the lodge.

The chef and his helper would be in the big kitchen, cooking a grand supper, and the maids would likely be off having doughnuts and coffee while they had the chance.

Dangerous, he thought. You get caught, you'll be on the run. From that bunch of organized profiteers, where could you even run?

Canada, maybe. Colder'n a Scotch maiden's crotch.

Mexico. Safer there and warmer, but a long ways to ride. Every telegraph office would be clicking, Wanted Dead or Alive, spreading the net.

You're not runnin', you're goin' to whip the murdering sonsabitches to doll rags. If you could just get some evidence to show a judge . . . the notebook . . .

Don't know if you can fool old Badger twice. Might not have even fooled him last night.

You got a big imagination, clown, he accused himself. Best take it as it comes, a step at a time.

When old white-haired Don Lyles finally hitched himself up on a slow-moving dun gelding, Badger Corbin let out his breath and growled, "Jesus H. Christ! We wait around much longer, it'll be dinnertime" and led the way out the gate northerly toward the mountains.

Reaching the timber, Badger pulled up and laid out the work.

"Clint, you go to the top. Curly, down from him a hundred yards. Shorty, another hundred yards down. Then me and Don can have the lower end. As we drive 'em, they'll likely head downhill, and when we get to Bengard Canyon, we'll turn and sweep 'em into the valley."

Clint had hoped he'd draw a spot farther down off the mountain, but it didn't make too much difference so long as he was going to leave anyway.

They rode up the mountainside, and the riders dropped off one at a time until only Curly was left, and when he turned, Clint said, "Give 'em hell, Curly," and continued on up through the junipers and pines until he was out of sight, then slanted back off the mountainside toward the ranch.

It was breaking every rule he lived by to turn his back on the job, and chances were he'd never be able to lie his way out of it, but overshadowing everything else was the yellow-haired Lee, his forehead burned black by the muzzle blast.

Coming in from the back to avoid Cooky or anyone else out in the yard, he rode down through the thick timber into a thicket of aspen and bear brush.

The place to look would be in the room they called the library, which also served as a central office, and as he came to the west side of the peeled-log lodge, he counted the windows from right to left. The shutters were hooked open, exposing the middle two windows that served the library.

Tethering the gray in the aspens, Clint worked his way to the log wall, took off his wide-brimmed Stetson, and raised his head to the level of the glass pane.

The floor was covered with rich buffalo robes, and varnished trophy antlers decorated the gleaming log walls. A long library table with six overstuffed chairs occupied the center of the room, and on either side of the great stone fireplace were shelves for books and file boxes. Clint put his thumbs under the window sash and pushed up. It didn't move. Locked by the simple hasp inside.

Moving on to the next window, he tried again. This time the frame yielded reluctantly, but once started, opened wide.

Hooking an elbow on the sill, he scrambled quietly inside.

The big, shining table was bare, the wastebasket empty, leaving only the file boxes next to the fireplace. He heard footsteps pass down the hall and froze as they slowed a moment at the library door and then passed on.

He smiled. The housekeeper probably decided she'd rather sit in the kitchen than dust elk horns.

Starting at the upper left-hand shelf, he opened file boxes and found long, detailed legal paper that he could barely decipher.

Impatiently he searched through the files, returning each box to the shelf in the same tidy shape he'd found it. Going to the other side of the fireplace, he looked through the remaining boxes with mounting frustration.

There was nothing. Only accounts of shipped cattle, prices, receipts, inventories, bids and contracts, but nothing important enough to murder a boy for.

Finishing with the last file box, he stepped back and looked at the center shelf, which was filled with books by Sir Walter Scott, Oliver Wendell Holmes, and William Ardmore Simms. Shaking his head in grim defeat, he caught sight of a notebook lying on top of the novels, only its shiny green spine showing.

Quickly he reached up for the green-cardboard-covered notebook on which was printed: Lee Durby.

There it was, not even hidden away, just put there so innocently he should have missed it.

He hurried toward the open window, but the book's potential information was too much to resist. Stopping in the light, he opened the cover to the first page.

Bronc peeler's chant I heard in the corrals:
"Git higher, git higher,
The higher you git is too low for me
Hang one spur where the collar works
And the other where the crupper works,
When I git back
There'll be a tornado!"

Leafing quickly on to the last page, he read:

Clint in jail and I'm the new beater!
Heard the senator telling the duke about
a hotel, a gambling casino, and a race-course out here. Impossible! Or is it?
I've wondered how they got all this beau-tiful country in the first place. Thought
it was homestead land. Check later.
They had a meeting out at the shooting
stand. Talked to a surveyor and signed

papers. Sure would like to get a peek. It's going to be a hard job to stop these pirates. They mean to steal the rest of the Crow Reservation! Wish big brother were here to help out.

That ended the catchall journal.

They must have caught him trying to get a peek. There was nothing much incriminating in these notes. Only suspicions. Hotel. Casino. Racecourse, but no solid evidence.

Riffling through the empty pages, a page of white hand-laid paper slipped loose and fluttered to the floor.

Reaching for it, he read the heading: Sawtooth Sporting Club.

Beneath that:

Memorandum of understanding

We, the owners of Sawtooth Cattle Syndicate, having completed the occupation of the Sawtooth River drainage containing approximately two hundred square miles, now agree to proceed with acquisition of the remaining Reservation and building the resort complex.

Using the natural assets of the area, such as the Cascade Cliff and unlimited fish, game, and wild fowl as basic attractions, we will construct hotels, racecourses, casinos, and hot mineral springs spas that will more than rival Saratoga Springs, New York.

Chicago-Seattle Railway will construct a track from Miles City, Montana, suitable for a luxury express passenger train.

Acquiring the land from the Crow Indians will be managed by Senator Cooley. The Department of Interior, Department of Army, and the Bureau of Indian Affairs will cooperate in clearing the area. Land to the depth of ten miles on either side of the tracks will be ceded to the Company as an incentive to build the railway.

Venture capital will be shared: Dorset Ltd. to provide 40%, the Ralston Bank of New York 40%, and Senator Cooley 20%, although shares will be distributed equally as recompense for the senator's special services in Washington on the Company's behalf.

Preliminaries begin immediately, and construction will follow as soon as possible. Signed:

Lorenzo Cooley
Percival, Duke of Dorset
C. James Ralston

"Interesting?" a feminine voice asked from the door.

So absorbed had he been in the memorandum, Clint hadn't heard the door open.

"I asked a question," the dark-haired lady said, closing the door carefully behind her.

"I was looking for my kid brother's notebook," Clint said, slipping the document back in the notebook.

As she moved closer, he realized she was the dark-haired lady dressed up in the Robin Hood costume of the day before.

"Then you're Clint Durby," she said. "I've heard of you and your brother."

She wore a simple cotton print dress today, and her dark russet hair had been left to hang down in natural waves to her shoulders. He glimpsed a trace of sympathy in her brown eyes.

"Came in the window?" she asked, seeing the obvious but showing no shock or concern.

"Yes'm. I thought you'd gone to town with the rest of them."

"They say you're a joker, never serious, but you look awfully serious to me."

"Ma'am, you can get me killed and I take that pretty serious." Clint smiled.

"Why should I say anything?" she asked simply. "I owe nothing to them."

"Nor me either, ma'am."

"My name is Emily Smith," she said.

"Smith's as good as any. Is that notebook evidence?"

"Of a kind," Clint said. "I aim to give it to Judge Chamberlain and let him figure it out."

"Mister Durby," she said, "they're too big for you or your judge. You'll just get yourself killed in an accidental shooting by men who never have accidents or make mistakes."

"Miss Emily, I got to try. You look a lot younger than I thought — why don't you try, too?"

"My daddy was a coal miner before he was crippled," she said slowly. "Now, with the senator's help, the family's doing better."

"You like the life?"

"No. I had other dreams, but poverty is poverty. The only way out is to sell what you have."

"Maybe you could get on your own out here."

"Too late." She tried to smile but failed.

"Think about it, Miss Emily," he said urgently. "I'll help you over the worst part —"

"And," she looked him square in the eyes, "at what price?"

Clint touched her shoulder with his free hand and answered honestly, "No charge."

"Maybe I'll take you up on it, Clint," she said softly. "If . . . you're still alive by the end of the week."

"I'm goin' to be more'n alive, Miss Emily. It's them others goin' to be in trouble."

"I hope so. I really do —" She hushed as they heard footsteps coming down the hall.

Clint slipped the hardbound notebook in his waistband and hurried to the window. As he bent over to go through, he felt her hand brush his cheek, then he was outside on the ground.

"I was just closing the window," she said to someone, sliding the sash down and turning away.

Clint made his way through the tangle of greenery to the gray, mounted up, rode clear of the ranch, then pulled up on a side hill.

He had to get the evidence to the judge, but the sheriff said the judge wouldn't be back until two days from now. Where could he hide the notebook until then, and hide himself too?

Working it out quickly, he figured if they didn't miss the book and they wanted to keep him under watch, he might as well swing around to the bunkhouse.

Staying in the timber until he was in sight of the barn and corrals, he halted the gray, unsaddled him, then using his jackknife, he frayed the twisted mohair strands of the girth until it fell apart. Working at the saddle, he forced the notebook in between the leather flap and the *basto* or saddle skirt, then led the gray into the yard and put him in the corral with the bay.

Carrying the saddle across the open yard, he saw Cooky come out of the cookhouse door and dump a dishpan of water.

"What you doin' back so early?" Cooky asked, surprised.

"Looks to me like some joker cut my girth," Clint growled, showing the frayed cinch. "Like to broke my neck when I fell."

"Where's the rest of the crew?" Cooky asked suspiciously.

"Hell, I couldn't catch 'em, and none of 'em came lookin', even if I rode bareback," Clint said angrily and bowlegged on to the bunkhouse.

Slamming the door, he hurried to his bunk with the saddle, and using the small blade of his Barlow, drilled a hole through the corner of the saddle's jockey flap and the skirt underneath, then found an old leather rosette he'd been saving and secured it over the hole with a leather thong that locked the hidden notebook in place.

After that, he went to work building a new cinch, half-hitching new mohair strings between the brass rings until he had fifteen strands side by side. Then he commenced weaving in the side bars and center bar with lighter material, whipping the ends smooth and finished.

He was finishing the center bar when Badger Corbin noisily stomped in, his wrinkled features flushed with anger.

"I'll be go to hell if you didn't jump the fence again," he rasped. "If I had my druthers I'd fire your butt out of here so fast you'd be squallin' like a turpentined cat!"

"What's got you so upset, Badger?" Clint smiled up at him. "You better pull on your ears to let the steam out."

"Why didn't you ride your place?" Badger snapped out, balling his fists.

Clint nudged the ruined cinch strands with his boot and said, "Take a look. I'd say they was mostly cut with a knife."

"Why in hell would anybody cut your cinch?"

"Maybe a practical joke or maybe the same reason my brother walked into a shootin' range, carrying his saddle," Clint said. "Maybe somebody cut his cinch, too."

"It couldn't be," Badger said heavily, letting out the pent-up breath from his lungs.

"I never did see that saddle. You sure he was carryin' it?" The hardness of Clint's stare belied his easy smile.

Badger flinched, and he looked across the room in a daze.

"Me? Did I say that?" he stammered. "I don't remember sayin' anything!"

"Don't get yourself a double hernia, Badger," Clint said more cheerfully. "Seems like I heard you boys buried the saddle with him."

"Yes, that's likely it." Badger nodded, looking away. " 'Course that's the way it was. Figured it was only right."

"Was the cinch cut?"

"No, I don't recollect it was . . ."

"Then we have to smoke out the jasper that cut my cinch and hang him by his thumbs till he squeals 'Uncle!' " Clint laughed.

"By God, you never take anything serious," Badger growled. "We been ridin' for Sawtooth three years together, and I thought I knew you to be an honest cowpuncher, but I ain't so sure anymore."

"Hell, you're just worryin' yourself raw as a skinned horse, Badger." Clint rose and clasped his long arm around the older man's slumped shoulders. "How come you're so spooky?"

"Yesterday the bay had a rock in his hoof, today it's a broke cinch. What'll you think of tomorrow?" Badger gritted out, staring at Clint.

"Don't fret yourself, old friend." Clint chuckled. "Like you said, we rode a lot of trails together. You don't hear me peckin' at where you been or where you're goin'."

"Ain't no reason to," Badger said, his face gray under the deep suntan.

"Where's the rest of the hands? Why ain't you out buglin' for them?"

Badger stopped, thought about it briefly, and relaxed. "Gosh damn, Clint, I seen the fire in your eyes and figured you thought I had somethin' to do with Lee's killin'."

"Naw, Badger," Clint said, dropping his eyes to the new cinch. "It's just I hate workin' my fingers to the bone, braidin' cinches."

"About time you bought a whole new rig." Badger slapped the polished seat of the saddle. "That old hull looks plumb wore out."

"If that's wore out, what do you think my butt looks like?" Clint laughed.

# CHAPTER 6

"Wake up, Jacob, day's abreakin', fryin' pan's on, and flapjacks bakin'!" Cooky's call, delivered always with the joy of disturbing others' pleasant dreams, elicited return greetings of mumbled curses, yelps, and groans as the older ones limbered up their joints for the day ahead.

Sitting at the long table in the cookhouse, Clint pushed his enameled tin plate aside, sipped the harsh, steaming coffee from a thick china mug, and asked, "What's on the hook for today, Badger?"

"I figure we'll fix up the breakin' corral before the boys bring in a band of wild ones," Badger said, still half asleep.

"I guess that way you can't get lost, Clint," Curly said, cocking an eye toward the tall puncher.

"I'll use the hammer and you can hold the spikes, Curly," Clint said.

"I dunno why —" Curly frowned.

" 'Cause I can see where to hit."

"Always got to be teasin' and playin' the idjit," Curly grumbled. "At least I can stay

103

on my horse and do my job."

"Sure you can, Curly." Clint got to his feet. "You're as good as they come around here."

"Now what's that supposed to mean?" Shorty demanded belligerently.

"What you so touchy about, Shorty? I didn't say he was better'n anybody." Clint smiled easily, going toward the door. "I swear a sackful of polecats has more joy in it than this cookhouse."

"Does anybody here believe a word he's sayin'?" Don Lyles said nervously. "He ain't jokin' — he's makin' it all up, teasin', tryin' to —"

"I think you're right, Don," Badger said, cutting him off, "but I can't make head nor tail of it."

"Whole crew's plumb gone barn sour," Clint said over his shoulder. "You all need a bottle of red-eye apiece and a waltz with Big-nosed Kitt. You done forgot how to hoot and howl."

Standing in the fresh, cool air, Clint glanced up at the rise where his brother lay. The jaunty angle of his stubbled jaw set, and the glittering mischief in his eyes turned to fire. Nodding to himself, he bowlegged it over to the tool-shed, picked out a six-pound hammer, and filled a pail with twenty-penny spikes from a keg.

"You better just take a shovel," Badger said from behind him. "I doubt you can wander too far from digging postholes."

"I aim to please," Clint said, taking a number-two shovel from a rack. "Not that I'm too chummy with an idiot stick. Always reminds me of grave robbers."

Badger winced, and his eyes turned quickly to see Clint's face. "How do you mean that?"

"My daddy always said to never get caught on the blister end of a shovel." Clint chuckled, rolling his eyes. "He said it'll come back to haunt you like a nightmare."

A film of sweat shone on Badger's lined forehead, and he growled, "I swear you're drivin' at somethin', but I don't know what."

"Steady on, old hoss." Clint winked at the older man. "It's a grand day for the livin', ain't it?"

"Cowboy," Badger said earnestly, "let me just tell you there's folks up at the lodge wouldn't take kindly to your way of passin' the time of day. They're different than us. They kill quick and they don't give a rat's ass about it, neither."

"You know that for a fact, Badger, or are you just tryin' to look serious while the bosses are watchin'?"

"I give you warnin'," Badger said as the others filed out of the cookhouse and moved reluctantly toward the toolshed.

"Speakin' of warnings," Clint murmured, hearing Mikowski's bellow from the steps of the lodge.

As Badger looked up, McLaglen and Tony Douglas came charging down the steps after Mikowski.

"What'd he yell?" Badger asked quickly.

"Said, 'hold up there!' I sure hope they've got fence buildin' on their minds."

The three men in their tight, wrinkled suits came trotting side by side across the yard as the crew waited.

"You reckon they're goin' to stampede right over the top of us?" Clint chuckled.

"Startin' right now, keep your mouth shut," Badger growled, facing the oncoming men.

"Hold it, right there!" Mikowski yelled again.

"We're makin' a search, startin' with you old farts," McLaglen growled, coming up close.

Clint leaned the shovel against the toolhouse and raised his hands.

"It's like the man said to his neighbor" — he grinned — "'I never borrowed your umbrella and if I did I brought it back again.'"

Without the slightest hesitation Tony Douglas yanked Clint's hat off, looked inside it, and tossing it on the ground, ran his hands under Clint's arms, down his back, and up his crotch.

"Ooooh, be gentle there."

"Get your boots off, the whole lot of you," the Cockney snapped.

Clint sat back on a sawhorse and, twisting and pulling, finally pulled the high-heeled boots free.

The Cockney ran his hand down the inside of each boot, and tossed them back to Clint. McLaglen had already searched Badger, and Mikowski finished with Cooky. Tony Douglas whirled Shorty around roughly, yanked off his hat, discarded it, and rapidly patted him down as McLaglen worked on Don Lyles.

"Mind tellin' me what this is all about?" Badger asked, his face flushed with anger.

"There's somethin' missin' from the house and we mean to find it," Tony Douglas said, his manner as matter-of-fact as a professional bounty hunter's.

"Maybe we can help," Badger said. "What is it?"

"It's a notebook with a green cardboard cover, about six by nine," McLaglen said, making measurements with his hands.

Every hand knew who had owned that notebook.

"I ain't seen it," Badger choked out. "We don't use a notebook much."

"We'll have a look," Tony Douglas said. "Stay here."

The three trotted toward the bunkhouse like wolves on the hunt.

Clint saw that by putting on the pressure quick and hard, they had the edge over everyone else. Fast, trained, hard-faced, they could keep a bunch of salty old cowboys off balance and treat them like yellow dogs.

Hearing the sound of bunks overturning and tables and chairs being thrown aside, Badger said grimly, "Goddamnit!"

"I'm drawin' my time," Curly said. "They's a hoo-doo on this place."

"I'm goin' with you, Curly," Shorty said. "Make mine out, too."

"You're too late." Clint chuckled wryly. "We're all too late."

"You can play the fool," Curly said, "but I'm leavin'."

"They won't let you go." Clint shook his head. "Nobody's goin' nowhere."

"Badger, you're ramrod," Shorty said. "You goin' to pay us off or not?"

"Not yet," Badger said. "Best wait a few more days."

"I ain't waitin'," Curly said, starting for the bunkhouse.

"Don't go in there, Curly," Clint said quietly. "You might have an accident."

"Accident? What do you mean?" Curly turned toward Clint.

"I mean we might find you drowned in a dishpan, somethin' like that."

Before Curly could reply, the three trained guards trotted out the bunkhouse door and on into the cookhouse, where Clint heard a mild protest from Cooky as he was flung aside. The sound of pans crashing and crockery breaking shattered the morning air.

Cooky shambled out, barefoot, his flour-patched face pale.

Sweating but still moving fast, the three hunters emerged from the cookhouse, trotted to the tack shed, and commenced throwing out saddles, bridles, cinches, odd straps and lead lines, halters and blinders, cans of bear grease and saddlesoap, hackamores, blankets and pads.

"Know their business, don't they?" Clint said to no one, seeing his saddle with its new cinch come sailing out the door and skidding into the dirt.

"Goddamnit!" Badger said tiredly, knowing he should take charge and stop the harum-scarum ransacking but knowing that he was afraid.

"Every cloud has a silver lining."

"Tell us what it is, you clown!" Badger turned on Clint fiercely, venting his rage and fear on the grinning cowboy.

"I figure we'll be so busy putting the wreckage back together, we won't be diggin' any postholes."

Emerging from the tack room, the three made short work of the blacksmith shop, which left only the barn with its bottom floor of horse stalls and the upper story a haymow that had never been used.

McLaglen looked up at the big building, hunched his heavy shoulders, and growled, "We got to do it."

In a moment, four horses were chased out into the corral and the sounds of the quick and intense search continued.

"After the barn, they got a couple hundred square miles of scenery to look over," Clint said.

"I don't care if I draw my pay or not," Curly said for show, "I'm ready to clear the hell out of here."

Red-faced and sweating, the three bodyguards returned from the barn, and Tony Douglas stood in front of Clint, tapped the butt end of a short quirt on his chest, and snapped, "Where is that notebook?"

"Gosh almighty," Clint beamed down at the shorter man, "nobody knows. Maybe you all buried it with the kid. We could dig him up if you'd like —"

In an invisible instant, the middleweight's left hook came out of nowhere and caught Clint just below the ribs.

He grunted as the air burst out of his lungs, and let the force of the blow carry him backward a step.

"Talkin' smart don't pay," the Cockney said plainly.

"My daddy always said a bug should never try arguin' with a rooster." Clint rolled his eyes.

"The old rummies don't know anything," McLaglen said harshly. "Better we take these two up to the lodge."

"Corbin could have an idea or two," Mikowski said, nodding heavily, "and the joker looks like a ringer to me."

"My Lord didn't say anything about bringing anybody to the main house," Douglas objected.

"We got to bring 'em something," McLaglen said, the Irish canniness in his eyes, "in case they get an idea it might be one of us . . ."

"Right you are." Douglas caught the message quickly. "Off we go."

"Get movin', Corbin, and you too, joker," Mikowski said, circling behind the two punchers.

"I always wanted a look-see in the big

house," Clint said, walking along with Badger, "but I just never thought I'd get a personal invite."

"Shut up," Badger said. "You're goin' to get us both killed."

"Oh, I'm dead set against that." Clint chuckled. "I'd rather they offered me a reward for finding that notebook."

"You know?" Badger whispered, looking up at Clint out of the corner of his eye.

"No, but I'd be willin' to look if they made the deal a little sweeter." Clint chuckled again.

"More of your foolishness," Badger growled disgustedly, and marched up the steps to the broad veranda.

Tony Douglas headed them toward the oak-paneled front door, opened it, and led the way through the vestibule into the main living room. It was furnished with settees and couches in front of a river-rock fireplace.

The three directors of the Syndicate sat at a large walnut table, each with a stack of papers in front of him.

"What have you found, Tony?" the duke purred softly.

"Sorry, Your Lordship, we turned the whole place upside down with no luck."

"It's our idea these two are the only ones smart enough to burgle the place," McLaglen put in.

112

"Where is it? I will not suffer disobedience or thievery," the blunt-headed banker growled at Badger.

Badger silently shook his head.

"Where were you yesterday?"

"Drivin' strays off the mountainside," Badger said.

"And this man?"

Badger hesitated a moment before making up his mind. "He turned up at the end of the gather."

"Where were you, Durby?"

"I was walkin' home. Somebody cut my cinch."

"He had the opportunity then," the duke said, pleased.

"Generally, if something's lost, you offer a reward for the findin' of it," Clint offered with a broad smile.

"You're that other Durby, aren't you?" bullnecked Ralston growled. "The one they call the joker. I suppose you could be foolish enough to challenge me."

"I was just talkin' about a reward —"

"The notebook was not lost, it was stolen," the senator declared, getting to his feet and pacing back and forth on his short legs. "If you return it promptly, we'll forget the whole matter and no questions asked."

"Mister," Clint said, "cowboys never steal

from their own brand."

"I daresay you can be persuaded to tell the truth," the duke said, his long horse face empty of emotion.

"Better talk to your three watchdogs. They all look like hooligans to me." Clint chuckled. "No offense, gents," he added, turning to face the three bodyguards.

"They have been tested," Big Jim Ralston growled, then glared at Senator Cooley. "Your woman was here yesterday."

The senator nodded. "That's true. Anything is possible at this moment."

"Get her," Ralston growled, and the senator trotted obligingly across the buffalo-robe rugs to the door.

"I can't see what's so dad-blamed important about the kid's notebook," Clint complained. "Heck, all he put in it was some cowboy songs and the yarns the old-timers like to tell —"

"Your brother was a good deal smarter than that," the duke said, "and a naughty boy too."

"Oh, he wasn't no hellion like me." Clint grinned. "I tried teachin' him, but he was slow to learn."

Before the duke could reply, the senator returned with Emily Smith. Clint held his crooked smile as he caught the fear in her eyes.

She wore a nightgown of lace and ruffles, covered by a long, lacy robe that she clutched to her throat as she looked from one man to the next, seeking a friend.

"Get Corbin out of here. It's not his game," Ralston barked, and McLaglen took Corbin's willing arm and headed him for the front door.

Ralston glared at Senator Cooley and said harshly, "The Syndicate comes first."

It was not a question, it was a direct command.

"Yes, Jim, I understand," Cooley said, not backing down. "It's always been that way with me."

"Sit down, then," Ralston growled and fixed his eyes on Emily. "Did you take the notebook? Just tell the truth and we'll indulge your mistake."

"No, sir, I didn't take it," she replied simply.

"What do you know about it?"

"I saw someone carry it into the lodge after the . . . accident," she said in a low voice. "After that, who knows?" She shrugged.

"You had the opportunity yesterday to prowl through the library," the duke said. "Suppose curiosity got the better of your good sense?"

"I had a headache yesterday. I stayed in my room."

"No, no, my dear" — the senator hopped to his feet and nimbly trotted to confront her

— "I found you in the library, remember?"

Emily's heart-shaped face paled slightly, but her features remained composed. "There was a draft. I went in to close the window."

"That's true," Cooley said, turning to Ralston. "She was closing the window when I came in."

Behind his cheery smile, Clint wondered if he'd left any boot tracks in the birch leaves below the window, and he was acutely aware that a search of the woods would reveal where he'd tethered the horse.

"Do you know this man?" the duke interrupted. "Look at him."

Emily looked Clint full in the face and after a long pause said, "No, he has some resemblance, though, to the dead boy."

"I'm his brother, ma'am," Clint said. "I keep sayin' these big fellas in the plug hats look guilty to me, but —"

"Enough!" shouted Big Jim Ralston, his face turning crimson, and Clint felt the back of a big hand smack across his mouth, staggering him with its force.

Standing in front of him, both fists ready to swing, McLaglen eyed Clint coldly.

"No offense, boys." Clint smiled crookedly, a trickle of blood curling down his chin.

"The notebook is at issue," Ralston said. "One or the other or both have it."

"Let's start with the woman." The duke smiled. "She looks so lovely just now . . ."

"I've told you all I know," Emily said strongly.

"My dear," the duke said, "we are acquainted with a Chinese gentleman in San Francisco who supplies us with cheap labor and in return, we supply him with common goods like you."

"Tell them, Emmy, and I'll see you get off," Cooley put in quickly.

"You know what they're threatening me with?" Emily said directly to the senator. "Would you permit that to happen?"

"Like I said," Cooley retorted, "the Syndicate comes first."

"I don't have the notebook and I don't know where it is," Emily said plain out, even as her chin trembled and her eyes went from one man to another.

"You had your chance." Senator Cooley stepped back to his chair and said, "McLaglen, persuade the misguided child."

"Here?" McLaglen asked, stepping forward.

"Of course." Cooley smiled. "It's better if she's among friends."

"Lady, you want a friend after this, look me up," Clint said quickly.

McLaglen looked down at Emily and

grinned. "You have the purtiest ears, only they don't quite fit your head right . . ."

Putting his doubled-up fists against each ear with his elbows wide, McLaglen pushed as if he meant to squeeze her head flat between his fists, and as he pushed with terrible strength, he ground his knuckles back and forth over her ears, milling them into broken cartilage and skin.

She shrieked once, her eyes rolled, and her slim body would have fallen to the floor had it not been held up by the pressure of the big Irishman's fists.

All eyes were on her until Clint growled, "You rotten son of a bitch!" and leaped forward, swinging as hard a right as he could throw at the plug-ugly.

Pain shot up to his elbow as McLaglen fell away, releasing Emily.

Rising, the big redhead came against Clint with both fists pumping, red rage in his bulging eyes.

Backing off, blocking McLaglen's fists with his arms and elbows, Clint smothered the flurry until a left cross grazed his ear. He countered with a hard hook to the soft belly of the big man, knocking the wind out of him.

Recovering quickly, McLaglen began a steady stalk, throwing roundhouse punches, trying to crowd Clint into a corner.

Aware of the danger of being caught with no room to dodge or retreat, Clint circled to the right, away from the power, looking for an opening when he could put his leverage into his own big right hand.

"A hundred dollars on the cowboy, Senator!" the duke called out, his eyes feverish.

"You're on!" the senator called back, and to Big Jim Ralston, "You want some?"

"I don't bet, I buy," Ralston rasped.

McLaglen, tiring from his earlier flurry and the thin air of the high plateau, came on doggedly, wasting his strength on haymakers that missed, until he started a left hand too slow.

Shifting his left foot forward, Clint drove off the toe of his right boot, his thigh muscles flowing into the momentum of his already arcing shoulder, snapping around, the force built up to maximum. Shoulder twisting, forearm striking out, the fist like a rock smashed against the point of the Irishman's jaw.

The force of the short punch snapped McLaglen's head around and he staggered backward, his eyes rolling. Pawing the air for support, he collapsed on the buffalo rug.

"An easy hundred, Senator!" The duke clapped his hands together excitedly.

"Stop this!" Ralston roared as Clint backed clear, his chest heaving for breath, eyeing Tony Douglas and Mike Mikowski as they

119

came at him from either side.

Mikowski muttered to Douglas and drove forward, his hands high to protect his face.

Clint stepped forward and kicked Mikowski in the crotch, then dived aside.

Too late, Clint realized he'd swerved into Douglas's path and saw before him the scarred, swollen eyebrows, the calm matter-of-fact eyes, saw the smaller man's shoulder shift, and felt the left jab smack his cheek. Trying desperately to get his left hand up to parry what he knew was coming, he felt the right-hand lightning bolt land on his jaw and smother the life in his brain.

# CHAPTER 7

The stone floor felt cool to his face, but his breathing wracked his chest and he wondered if he was having a bad dream and waking up or if he was just moving from one nightmare to another in a long, hard night.

Trying to ease the pain in his chest, he rolled over on his side and heard a voice echoing through the cobwebs of his mind. "He's coming out of it."

"The notebook . . . where is it?" a crisp British voice faded in and faded away again.

"Give him some more!"

Clint brought his arm down to protect his bruised ribs, and a shriek of agony broke from his lips as the boot slammed into his kidney.

"The notebook . . . where is it?"

It's against the law to kick a man when he's down, Clint thought foolishly and smiled at his own craziness.

"He likes it!" a rougher voice came through.

As Clint moved his arm down over the kidney area, a boot came in from the side and smacked against his aching ribs.

"The notebook . . . where is it?"

121

Another boot to the thigh this time sent him flopping over onto his swollen, bloody face.

"Keep at it, but don't kill him." The crisp diction echoed through the convolutions of his mind until the darkness came again . . .

. . . A mumbling of distant voices, a scraping of chair legs on stone, the smell of burning coal oil in a lamp, voices coming clearer as he lay sprawled on the floor.

"Beat him any more, he'll be a permanent dummy . . . won't ever know nothin' . . . there's other ways . . ."

"Pour boilin' grease in his ear — that'll get his attention . . ." Hoarse guffaws . . .

"Let me go get a skillet . . ."

"Go ahead, I'm goin' outside and take a leak."

"Piss in his ear after I pour the boilin' oil in . . ."

The hoarse guffaw again . . . the British accent . . . the door opening . . . closing . . . silence . . .

Clint opened one eye and saw the flat limestone. He turned his neck, and like an animal emerging out from the depths of swamp, his mind slowly cleared as he hitched his aching bones together and got to his knees, knowing it was now or never. . . .

Vision swimming, his thinking dull and slow, he looked about and saw the lighted

122

lamp sitting on a pine kitchen chair and nothing else in the room.

The door was made of solid pine planks; iron brackets on both sides were meant to hold a two-by-four bar that leaned in the corner.

Why bar inside, he wondered blearily . . . Who knows . . . maybe they buried their bodies under the stone floor . . . maybe they counted their money . . . maybe they tortured their women . . .

Mikowski would be coming back with the hot oil — it wouldn't take much to burn the insides of a man's brain into raw agony . . . Hurry up, clown . . . now or never . . .

No weapon, not even his old Barlow jackknife left . . . He can snap your neck with two fingers . . . On your feet, funny man . . .

Holding on to the timbered wall, Clint climbed to his feet and hung on as a spiraling dizziness sent him weaving back and forth, trying to find his balance.

He tried the door, pulling on the china knob, but it wouldn't budge . . . barred on the outside . . . the bar . . . the bar . . . He lifted the two-by-four and dropped it into the iron brackets, then took a deep breath that almost doubled him up with pain.

Now what? He can't get in, you can't get out.

The lamp . . . the chair . . . nothing else . . .

Setting the lamp carefully on the floor, he tried to think a plan through, but his brain was so lost in meaningless haze, he lost his train of thought twice before he could get the pieces lined up in his head. . . .

Fire . . . fight . . . run . . .

The rickety chair splintered against the stone floor and Clint made a pile of kindling in the far corner, then leaned back against the door, gaining strength, his head clearing from the small exertion. His left hand trembled uncontrollably from nerve damage, and every half minute or so a spasm of shuddering would start somewhere in his midsection, vibrating his whole body, then passing on.

Be quick, Clint . . . Panamint Clint . . . Clown . . . No more . . . growin' up . . .

He shook his head as he heard heavy boots coming down wooden steps . . . Ready, Clint?

The boots scraped on the stone floor outside and Clint, in simple despair, threw the glass lamp onto the little pile of chair scraps, stepped back from the sudden blaze, lifted the two-by-four from the brackets, and moved aside with his back to the wall.

The door opened and big Mike Mikowski, carrying a small, smoking skillet, saw the blaze and yelled, "Holy Christ!"

As he rushed to kick out the fire, Clint set himself and swung the length of the two-by-four, with all the power left in him, square against the back of the man's head.

The crunch had a wet sound to it, and Clint felt the give in the heavy skull.

Mikowski's bulk hurtled through the smoke and his head plowed into the stone wall above the blaze. Collapsing into the fire, he didn't even scream at the agony of his burning face. Dead men don't whimper.

Clint tossed the club aside, dragged the mountainous bulk from the fire, and found a small Navy Colt in a holster under the coat. He kicked the remnants of the fire to smoldering embers, closed the door behind him, and sucked clean air free of the stench of burned meat and hair.

Where was he? Where was he going?

He was in the basement and he wanted out.

Holding the .36-caliber six-gun ready in his right hand, he climbed the wooden steps in the darkness.

He had no idea of how long they had worked him over, but it wasn't dawn yet. There was no sound in the house except the creak of timbers settling against each other.

He found a hall and a door.

There was another man somewhere. Supposed to be taking a leak. He'd be outside, just standing around now, maybe watching the stars before coming back to the dirty job of pouring boiling hot oil into a cowboy's brain.

He could be near this door. . . .

Holding to the darkness, Clint silently turned the knob, gave it a pull, and stepped to one side, letting it swing open.

"That you, mate?" came the Cockney accent.

Clint saw the shadow on the stoop and came forward whispering, "Yeah, it's me . . ."

Moving closer, he lunged and struck with the revolver at Tony Douglas's head.

The middleweight's reflexes were trained to dodge, and the force of the blow was softened by his falling away.

Clint charged quickly, struck twice more, each blow connecting somewhere on the pug's head; the third one dropped him like a sack of corn.

One for the money! Clint smiled crazily. Two for the show, three to get ready, and four to go!

With that, he lashed the revolver down once more against the side of Douglas's bare skull.

Growin' up, he thought bitterly. He walked painfully across the yard to the tack shed, located by feel his saddle and bridle, and carried them to the corral, where he hoped to Christ one of his string was waiting.

The leggy gray and the bay were both in the holding pen, both so gentle they didn't need to be roped.

Blanket and hull on the bay's back, bit in his mouth, and with every joint howling for relief, Clint hoisted himself into the saddle and let the bay shuffle across the yard to the big log gate, pass on to the moonlit wagon trace, then lift to an easy trot toward town.

He'd hit Douglas the fourth blow in order to gain time and distance from the ranch. But where was he going?

No, he thought, you can't get justice by hidin'. You get justice by fightin' for it. Find the judge. Clint remembered Sheriff Cox saying the judge would soon be back in town.

Would a judge believe him? They likely would fix it up so that Mikowski's death looked like murder. Man was hit in the back of the head with a two-by-four, looks like cowardly murder to me, Clint mused.

They'd probably explain how Mikowski's face was half burned off, saying that Clint Durby was a hellhound, had tortured the poor fella, laughing like a fiend while he was doin' it.

As he rode along, a special stillness came over the long valley and a faint, luminous glow diluted the darkness over the eastern scarps.

They'd been beating on him off and on most of the night, he realized, but he could remember only pieces of it, the focusing of his swollen eyes, the boot, then the returning darkness. Why?

Sure they wanted the book, especially that memorandum, but why were they so desperate for it? Why not just kill him and let the papers stay hidden? Unless they were afraid of what he might have already done with them, Clint speculated. If the Indian lovers back east got wind of what the Syndicate aimed to do to the Crow Reservation, the whole scheme would fall apart.

That's why they'd wasted no time hunting down Lee before he could return to Chicago. They couldn't possibly let him go on living, knowing what he knew.

With me, it's different, he thought. They didn't worry about me because I don't know anybody back east, especially anybody who could put this stuff in an honest newspaper. So I don't count much, as long as they get back the notebook and memorandum. Only one I know can put the kibosh on 'em is Judge Chamberlain. Wonder if they'd go so far as to kill him too? Likely. They make their own laws.

Still, I reckon I'm goin' to try. Like Daddy always said, we will try, do or die. With him it was mostly die after the mule gave out. Plowed up a hell of a lot of sod with that mule, but forgot to put up a sign sayin': All Grasshoppers Keep Out.

Stop it, clown — Clint chided himself — you're growin' up.

*You'd make the best cattleman in Montana if you'd just grow up....*

The eastern Absarokas limned like giants against the screen of rosy fire filled with speckly orange embers boiling up from the lifting sun, and he stopped by the stream to wash the blood off his face and hands, the blood and bile from his mouth.

The thudding in his head diminished and he felt more like a man as he mounted again and put the bay into an easy canter, now that they could see the ground clearly.

How did old Badger fit into this scheme? Clint concluded he didn't. He was just caught by time and circumstances and couldn't see any reason for taking a step into the cold dark so long as he could hold his job.

Badger wasn't so dumb he wouldn't know what was going on, but as long as he didn't see it, then he could have a clear conscience. He'd be loyal to the brand, and among cowboys in general, you couldn't do any better.

Would he have stood still for McLaglen punishing Emily Smith so cruelly? He might, by assuming she was a shady lady working for the brand just like everybody else.

Like the senator had said, "The Syndicate comes first."

Didn't make any difference if it was rotten clean through to murder, just so it made money.

What would happen if everybody in the Company said, No, my conscience comes first and I want the rottenness rooted out from top to bottom?

Wouldn't that be grand!

Poor damn Indians'd keep their rightful land and brand their own beef and make their magic in their sacred hot springs, and Saratoga could keep right on taking the millionaires' money.

You're thinkin' crazy, he told himself. Empty stomach's givin' your head the blind staggers.

What you ought to be puttin' your puny mind to is how close are the Sawtooth riders. Them mighty three ain't goin' to be standin' around mourning Mikowski, they're goin' to be runnin' you down, soon as they figure out which way you went.

The sun was a red ball over the scarps and peaks by the time Clint reached town and reined up in front of Ike's Cafe.

Much as he didn't want to show his battered face, he felt like he'd fall down if he didn't eat. And he sure couldn't fight if he was weak from hunger.

Old peg-legged Ike surveyed Clint's ruined

countenance, put a mug of coffee in front of him, clucked his tongue, shook his head, and asked, "What happened?"

"Husband come home unexpected and I fell out the upstairs window," Clint said. "How about six eggs straight up and a batch of bacon and fried spuds?"

"Coming up," Ike said, not smiling, and pegged back into the kitchen.

Clint thanked providence that the cafe was empty. Folks is always extra curious about a beat-up cowboy.

"How's things at Sawtooth?" Ike called through his serving window.

"So-so," Clint said.

"I'm sorry about your brother. Made me sick when I heard the news."

Clint nodded and said, "We're born to die."

"Couple of 'em rich dudes was in yesterday. Took over the telegraph office, and no one could get in for two hours. They better tone up their manners or folks'll be down on 'em."

"Do you think they give a rat's ass?" Clint asked mildly.

"Likely not, but things run a lot better if there's some kindness and respect in the mix," Ike muttered, bringing the breakfast platter to the counter.

Filling Clint's coffee mug again, Ike stood

131

there, his face troubled.

"I just don't know anymore," he said, shaking his head. "This used to be a pleasant enough town, but lately it's changin'. Folks along Main Street are tryin' to grab the money like it might not be around next week."

"What's that old sayin' about bad money always drivin' out the good?" Clint said.

"That's it. But I don't see where it's gone bad."

"I reckon you can see that Sawtooth is the rotten apple in the barrel," Clint said, scrubbing his plate with a piece of sourdough bread. "Sheriff in town?"

"He's gettin' so old, he don't travel much anymore." Ike picked up the platter and put it on the serving shelf. "None of my business, but what are you wantin' him for?"

"Advice," Clint said, rising and laying a quarter on the counter. "Much obliged. I feel strong as a wild mountain bull now."

"Advice?" Ike croaked as the door closed behind Clint.

Walking down the street toward the sheriff's office, Clint debated on how much to tell and how much not to tell.

What he needed was guidance from somebody who was experienced in law problems, and Sheriff Cox was the only one he was acquainted with.

Whatever he was going to do or say, he was going to have to do it before the Sawtooth riders picked up his trail and sent word back that they had the coyote denned.

He found Sheriff Cox in a tilted-back oak chair with his gaiters up on the desk, cleaning his Peacemaker with a piece of oily cloth.

Seeing Clint's mashed features, he set his feet down on the floor and said, "Your face looks like a blacksmith used it to shoe a mule. Who you been in a scrap with this time? Somebody who didn't think one of your jokes was funny?"

"I went out of the joke business," Clint said, "I got somethin' else on my mind."

"Shoot," the sheriff said, leaning over the desk toward Clint, his frosty eyes alert.

"First off, Lee wasn't killed accidental. He was murdered by the three boss dudes out at Sawtooth."

"You got proof, son?" the sheriff asked. "I'd hate to think Badger and the senator lied to me."

"Badger was just repeating the lie they told him," Clint said, trying to tell what happened in a way that made sense.

". . . Lee's saddle was still cinched on his dead horse when I found it up a little side valley. I found three separate places they had hid to shoot the horse, then Lee. He was hit three times, the last one about an inch from his head."

"How do you know that?" The sheriff's lined face was troubled.

"I dug him up and looked. It couldn't have been an accident with the killshot that close."

"Somethin' don't sound square," the sheriff murmured. "Why would them three be after the boy?"

"He took some evidence they couldn't stand for anybody to have," Clint said. "He must've had it with him, otherwise they wouldn't have killed him so fast."

"What sort of evidence?" the sheriff asked, looking away doubtfully.

"A document Lee put in his notebook, I reckon," Clint said. "That's how I got scratched up."

"You have the notebook?"

Clint paused a moment before answering, thinking that in truth, that notebook was the only thing keepin' him alive, and it was the only real weapon he had to bring down the whole Sawtooth organization.

"No," he said, adding, "Maybe I could find it, just maybe."

"Without some proof, there's only your word against theirs," the sheriff said, shaking his head.

"They're goin' to be in here pretty quick

wantin' my head on a platter," Clint said. "I'm tryin' to be legal and right at the same time."

"You hurt somebody out there?" the sheriff asked quietly.

"One of them big bodyguards that booted me around all night."

"Why'd they do that, for Christ's sake?" The sheriff let his temper show.

"They want that notebook mighty bad. They've also got one of their women locked up, if she's still alive. Name of Emily Smith."

"A woman plays in that game she has to look out for herself," the sheriff said. "Now where's this notebook and how bad did you hurt the man?"

"I reckon the hardcase is dead. As for the notebook, I'm hopin' I can steer it to Judge Chamberlain, soon as he gets back."

"I ain't said yes or no yet, Clint," the sheriff said slowly. "I'll tell you this, though — there's nobody else in this town you can trust except me."

"Did I say I didn't trust you?" Clint started for the door.

As he reached the door, he heard the Peacemaker's hammer click back.

"You ain't goin' nowhere just yet, Clint," Sheriff Cox said softly.

Clint turned to see the six-gun aimed at his chest and held with a steady hand.

"Put that little hideout Colt down on the floor and kick it over here," the sheriff said coldly.

After Clint had skidded the Navy Colt across the scarred pine floor to the desk, the sheriff said, "Now, just go on down to your old cell and make yourself comfortable."

"You goin' to turn me over to 'em?" Clint asked bitterly.

"I'm goin' to get to the bottom of this business." The sheriff smiled. "Looks to me that I'm holdin' ace high."

Followed by the sheriff, Clint moved down the hallway into the cell and sat on the bunk. "Can't you just wait till the judge comes and let him settle it?"

"Don't fret your mind about the judge." The sheriff smiled. "You just confessed to a murder out at the ranch. I'll make sure justice is done."

"You sold out to them already?" Clint asked.

"Not yet" — the sheriff chuckled — "but let me tell you something, I used to be a respectable gunfighter down along the border twenty years ago. I enjoyed those times because things was simple. A man calls your hand, you go for your gun. That made sense to me and I enjoyed it in good health until I started slowin' down."

"So you took up bein' a lawman?"

"And even that ain't permanent. Folks are already lookin' for some bright young feller that can serve papers and work cheap."

"What are you drivin' at?"

"If you live long enough, you'll figure that every man, when he reaches a certain age, better start lookin' to his future. What I'm lookin' for is a steady pension so I won't have to be beggin' on the street. That ain't much to ask after a lifetime, is it?"

"Depends on the lifetime," Clint said as the sheriff locked the iron-barred door. "If it never amounted to more'n a plugged nickel, that's about what it's worth. You a lawman or not?"

The sheriff stopped and glared at Clint. "Listen, joker, you better learn, in the time you have left, there's two sets of laws — the ones the rich make for the poor, and the ones the rich make for the rich."

# CHAPTER 8

"Sheriff Cox, now he's a hard man," Deputy Arbuckle said, hitching his belt up over his belly, shaking his head, peering at Clint through small, narrow-set eyes. "Killed I don't know how many men down on the border."

Easing his thin shanks down on the chair next to Clint's cell, his gaunt features set in deeply serious lines, Arbuckle added, "He means to sell your hide to the top bidder."

"I've got that much figured out already."

"Now, with me it's different," Arbuckle said seriously. "I swore to uphold the law and that's what I try to do, no matter what the sheriff tells me."

"I just want to give Judge Chamberlain the evidence and let him handle the rest of it."

"I'm glad you're not talkin' revenge. A man talkin' revenge against the big money is like a grasshopper goin' after a lizard."

"I want justice for Lee," Clint said, wondering why the skull-faced deputy was wasting his time jabberin' like a jaybird.

"I'm on your side, Clint, always have been,"

Arbuckle said intently. "I never saw no harm in any of your fool pranks. I tried tellin' Cox that maybe you was just a little harum-scarum, but you'd grow out of it soon enough."

"Thanks," Clint said, although he couldn't remember a time when Arbuckle had ever done him a favor.

"Cox is a man who went to killin' down on the border and never got over it. I've got different ideas. I say you have to treat a man fair and square. Ain't that right?"

Clint felt a prickly sensation on the back of his neck and thought, What does he want?

"Right as rain," Clint said, waiting it out.

"The world's got to change," Arbuckle sighed, wiping the sweat off his bulging forehead. "We ain't a pack of animals anymore. Montana will be a regular state in the Union in a year or two. It ain't right to have a gunfighter with blood on his hands bein' sheriff."

"You want to fill his boots?" Clint said, nodding.

"I ain't pushing too hard, but I'm the right man for the job."

"You suppose there's a building in this town or even a town lot that's not owned by Sawtooth Cattle Syndicate?" Clint asked.

"The sheriff did come in about the same time Sawtooth took over from the Injuns . . ."

"I 'spose if the big three said string a man

139

up, folks in town'd do it," Clint said, frowning.

"Not if I was in charge," Arbuckle said firmly. "I'd defend your rights same as I would anybody's else's; that includes the right to keep on breathin'. Once Henry Arbuckle is sheriff, there won't ever be another lynchin' in this town, I can promise you that."

"I'll vote for you, Arbuckle," Clint said, "if you can keep me alive till election time."

"That might not be so easy." Arbuckle sighed, pursing his thin lips thoughtfully. "I don't have much of a say-so just now."

"You mean there's no hope?" Clint asked, knowing there was a large spider spinning a web inside of Arbuckle's bony head.

"I'd have to go up against the sheriff," Arbuckle said. "He may be gettin' a little mossy-backed, but he's still stewed-down lightnin' with that hair-trigger Peacemaker."

"I wouldn't ask you to do that, but I ought to have a fair chance against him."

"How do you mean?" Arbuckle asked, his eyes studying the floor, his voice low.

"If I had a gun, it'd at least be a fair fight," Clint said, "and if I downed him, you'd be elected."

"No, your reputation is too much on the fiddlefoot side, skylarkin' and jokin' and such, for people to believe you. I'd be blamed for

arming a prisoner. We both know that, Clint."
Arbuckle seemed to be pleading with Clint
to come up with a way of saving his own life.

"You got something else on your mind?"
Clint asked harshly.

"What about that notebook? With evidence
like that to back us up, we'd both come out
on top," Arbuckle said.

"Lee's notebook? Sure, but I'm savin' that
for the judge," Clint said slowly, seeing the
threads of Arbuckle's web coming together.

"Just tell me where it is as an act of good
faith, and I'll give you the key and the gun,"
Arbuckle said.

"There's nobody can lay hands on that
notebook except me." Clint shook his head.

"You're willin' for me to be fired or killed
or both, but you don't trust me," Arbuckle
said, disappointed.

"What I want is justice for Lee, whether
I live or die. You'd have to promise me that."

"I promise on my mother's gravestone,"
Arbuckle said softly. "I'll make sure the judge
gets that notebook, or die tryin'. That suit
you?"

Clint paced the floor as he reckoned that
he didn't really know Arbuckle except as a
sort of flunky doing odd jobs. Maybe he was
a bigger man inside than people gave him
credit for.

"Clint, we haven't got much time," Arbuckle said.

"Got me in a nutcracker," Clint sighed, nodding his head. "I just hope you won't let me down."

"You can count on me like I was your brother," Arbuckle said strongly.

Clint looked at him — the pinched-in pig eyes, the bony chin stubbled and greasy — and thought, I'd never have a brother that looked like that . . .

"Step right in, gents, and see the killer!" Sheriff Cox called out, opening the door and leading two bowlegged, stiff-jointed punchers down the hall.

Putting on a tight smile, Arbuckle stood and asked, "Everything all right, Sheriff?"

"Sawtooth's lookin' for this gent," Cox said, poker-faced.

Tall old Curly and low-slung, thin-boned Shorty stared at Clint through the bars, observing the cuts and bruises on his face, saying nothing.

"Boys," Clint said, "it came down to him or me, and I was luckier."

"We was told you picked a fight with Mikowski," Curly said, his rheumy eyes wandering.

"Then, after he licked you fair and square, you sneaked up from behind and broke his

142

headbone," Shorty said in his slow, south-Texas drawl.

"Makes sense," Curly said.

"It wasn't that way. I've got Lee's notebook and they tried to sweat it out of me," Clint said.

"Where is it?" Shorty asked softly.

"I can't tell till I talk to the judge," Clint said anxiously. "I'm tryin' to do the right thing."

"You're goin' against the brand," Curly said, shaking his gnarly old head. "Anybody'd rob the boss's house would do anything."

"It ain't a brand," Clint said sharply. "It's a goddamned syndicate of skunks that mean to steal the whole damn Territory."

"I liked you better when you was a joker," Shorty said.

"Just like I said," Cox put in. "The damn fool wants to give the country back to the Injuns."

"Find the senator's lady, Emily Smith — she'll tell you," Clint came close to pleading.

"She's gone. They say she pilfered the senator's wallet while he was sleepin'," Curly said.

"That kind of woman would," Shorty added.

"She wouldn't," Clint retorted. "She just knows too much."

"Best you gents tell your bosses I'd like to have a little talk," Cox said.

"Why not just come on out and have your talk?" Curly asked.

"I reckon it'd be safer if I stayed and guarded my prisoner," the sheriff said smoothly.

"Anything we can do for you, Clint?" Curly asked.

"Have pity on my horse and give him a bait of grain," Clint said after a moment, "and then stay clear when the fireworks start, because I'm gettin' some riled 'bout this short deck of cards."

"I give you credit for thinkin' about your horse," Shorty said, "but for the rest of it, you ain't never been right in the head."

"Give those three gents my message right off," the sheriff said as they filed down the hall.

"Hold your water. They won't be rushin' to town this late in the day," Curly muttered.

"Tell 'em I'm waitin' at the Calico Queen," Sheriff Cox said, closing the hall door and going along with them.

"Mighty close," Arbuckle whispered after a long silence. "Tell me where you hid that notebook and I'll get you out of here."

"I don't think you can handle those hombres," Clint said.

144

"I reckon you don't trust me," Arbuckle said heavily, rising to his feet.

"No offense, Arbuckle," Clint said quickly, "it's just I've got the one chance to make good for my brother, and I don't want to miss it."

"I was volunteerin' my help. If you don't want it, it's no hide off my butt," Arbuckle said as he left.

Dang it, Clint thought bitterly, he's mad too. Likely the only friend you got in this town, and you just lost him.

*You'd be the best cattleman in Montana if you'd ever grow up. . . .*

Dang it, Lee, I'm tryin'! I just can't do nothin' about iron bars!

In his mind he saw Lee smile and nod confidently, like he was saying, Don't fret overly much, you'll figure it out.

Clint lay back on the bunk and tried to think of anything he might have overlooked that could break him loose.

Nothing.

When Arbuckle returned from Ike's Cafe with Clint's supper, Clint thanked him and sipped at the coffee, nibbled without appetite at the bacon, and ate some of the beans just to be doing something.

"I sugared the coffee for you, Clint," Arbuckle said.

"I generally don't like it sweet," Clint said, "but I'm much obliged to you."

"Dark out already," Arbuckle said. "Won't be long till mornin'."

"I can't figure out your meanin'."

"I'm askin' for the last time. Tell me where the book is, and I'll give you the key and the gun. Yes or no?"

"They'd just cut you to pieces like they done me," Clint murmured.

"By now the sheriff's half asleep over at the Queen and most of the town's gone to bed," Arbuckle said absently, studying his bony hands. "That just leaves you and me."

"I ain't too eager to play any checkers," Clint said tiredly.

"I been thinkin' about a horse I had once. Good-lookin' son of a bitch, but he'd never behave. A broncbuster could ride him down so he was gentle as a treeful of possums, but whenever I'd get close, he'd kick and bite, tryin' to savage me."

"Best you traded him off."

"I didn't do that, Clint. I tied him in a stall and then I took a length of loggin' chain to him." Arbuckle smiled, remembering. "Worked up quite a sweat, whippin' that horse with the chain. I whipped his tail off at his butt. I whipped his eyes out, and I whipped his teeth out, and I whipped his hide

146

off so he looked like a skinnin' lesson. Then the son of a bitch died on me."

"Can't blame him much," Clint said, moving back to sit on the bunk as a strange lassitude pulled him down.

"Be back in a minute," Arbuckle said, and going into the office, returned with a four-foot length of chain and the big iron key to Clint's cell.

"I tell you, Clint, old friend, I want that book and what's in it."

Clint tried to get to his feet, but his left boot went the wrong way and he staggered drunkenly against the wall.

"Why?" Clint asked through dry lips, his eyes blurring, the cell slowly rotating.

"I want to be like one of them Syndicate stockholders so they just mail me my pay every month. Now, I ain't beggin' anymore. Where is it?"

"What'd you put in that coffee?" Clint asked thickly, swaying to keep his balance as his eyes tricked him.

"Whole bottle of laudanum." Arbuckle grinned. "Tincture of opium makes you sleepy, don't it? Warm and cozy."

"Not me." Clint clutched at the bars to keep from falling.

"While you're feelin' nice and dreamy-like, Clint, tell me about the notebook, how you found it, what all's in it."

"I found . . . it . . . ," Clint slurred drowsily, "in the . . . library . . . the memo . . . signed . . ."

"Then what did you do with it, Clint, old friend?" Arbuckle asked softly, his eyes bright and fixed on Clint's twisted features.

"I dunno . . . where . . . put somewhere . . ."

"Think about it, old friend," Arbuckle coaxed. "Think back on what you did with it."

". . . Can't . . . ," Clint said groggily. "What . . . ?"

"The notebook, Clint. Where is it?" Arbuckle tried to hide his impatience and stood to face Clint. "Think!"

"Notebook . . . ," Clint murmured, his brain going round and round in shadows and light, with some inner voice warning him to play dumb. "Don't . . . know . . ."

"Sure you know, Clint," Arbuckle wheedled. "You took it from the library and you put it someplace where we could find it."

"Oh Susan Van Dusan . . . ," Clint sang laboriously, but with a big smile on his blank face,

> "Oh, I'll quit my tobacco
> And boozin'
> For you'n . . ."

"Goddamn it to hell, you fool! You know! Now tell me!" Arbuckle snarled, losing control.

"I'm goin' to waltz my Susan . . . ," Clint said, lurching toward the bunk.

"Like hell!" Arbuckle unlocked the door and, grabbing up the chain, brought it up from the floor over his shoulder and caught Clint across his back with its whipping end.

"No!" Clint howled, feeling the shock and pain of the iron links tear into his back.

"Wake up, Clint! Think! Where?"

From some adrenaline source deep inside came a new clarity to Clint's mind, and he staggered away to the far corner of the cell. "No more!"

Arbuckle took a step forward and lashed out again with the chain, numbing Clint's left shoulder and driving him to his knees.

"Wake up, Clint! Tell me where you put it," Arbuckle grated, dragging the chain back. "I popped out his eyes. I broke out his teeth . . ."

"No. I can't . . . don't!" Clint cried out, trying to get to his feet, trying to find some strength left in his rubbery arms and legs.

"Once more . . ." Arbuckle grinned, a wild sadistic light in his eyes, and lunging forward, he brought the chain crashing down on Clint's fending arm and across the back of his head.

Desperately Clint clutched at the chain's end with his right hand, the links tearing through his nerveless fingers, until he whirled the hand and got a loop of chain wrapped around his wrist.

Arbuckle pulled back hard and fast, but Clint had the dally around his wrist and hung on as the links bit into his hand, the pain clearing the hazy scud from his brain.

Because of that pain, Clint was momentarily the stronger, and with a flush of desperate strength, he jerked the chain free from Arbuckle's hands.

Arbuckle stolidly thought it over, eyeing the slumped cowboy, weighing his chances. He could back out the door and lock it or he could use his gun as a club.

Drawing the Colt, he lunged forward and swung at Clint's head. Clint dodged and blindly swung the chain in an arc that smacked Arbuckle's right elbow, knocking the six-gun free.

Arbuckle scrabbled for the gun with his good left hand, found it, and rose with a crooked smile on his pale, hollowed face.

Clint staggered forward and, with both hands, whirled and brought the chain up from the floor, angling to strike at the .44.

As Arbuckle saw the blur of chain he ducked aside, and the bight of iron slammed the base of his skull, and wrapped around the scrawny neck to make a double loop that didn't come free as Clint jerked the thin man toward him.

Arbuckle collapsed, his face turning the color of thick tallow. His lips vainly sucked for air, and his pinched chest wracked spasmodically.

Blearily Clint saw the chain links driven deep into the neck, but he was past thinking, past caring.

Arbuckle's back arched as his fingers mindlessly played at loosening the chain, and with bulging eyes and a rictus of death opening his lizard lips wide, he collapsed to the floor.

The only thought in Clint's drugged, disordered mind was to run. *Run! Now! Now!*

# CHAPTER 9

Going on instinct alone, Clint staggered up the hall to the office where a lamp wick guttered, found his gunbelt and .44 hanging on a peg behind the desk, slung them over his shoulder as he passed by, and lurched out the front door to the dark boardwalk.

Across the street in front of the Calico Queen, a few patient ponies stood at the hitchrail, heads down, sleeping on their feet.

The saloon remained quiet as Clint, one hand touching the building fronts, made his laborious way down the boardwalk. Crazily, he thought they needed a clown in there to liven things up. . . .

His mind drifted in and out of blackness, and at the corner he fell to his knees. Too weak to climb to his feet, he crawled in the darkness until he bumped into a hitchrail that served as a handhold. On his feet again, he staggered on, thinking only, Away . . . Away . . .

Again his mind went blank and he fell. The rank smell of garbage told him that he was still close to human habitation, and as he tried to get to his feet again, his left leg gave way. Collapsing against a flimsy door frame, he lay there, trying to get the good in and the bad out.

Soon dawn would light the streets.

Got to git . . . he told himself, and as he tried to grip the door frame, he knocked his head against the thin panel.

"Who is it?" came a drowsy feminine voice from inside.

Clint tried to crawl away, but his body wasn't answering the commands coming from his brain.

The door opened inward and he fell half inside.

"Who is it?"

A moment later a lamp glowed through the doorway and a black-haired woman in a nightgown leaned over the helpless cowboy.

"Clint?" she whispered in astonishment. "Clint, what the hell happened to you!"

He turned his head painfully until he could look at the face of Ruby Campbell.

Unable to speak, he shook his head slowly and closed his eyes.

The sporting girl put the lamp on a table, leaned down, and taking Clint by the shoulders, dragged him inside. She quickly closed and barred the door.

The room was tiny and taken up mostly

by the rumpled bed and the washstand on which sat an ewer of water in a white ironstone basin.

"Help me, Clint," Ruby whispered as she tried to lift his shoulders onto the bed.

He rolled out of her hands, but slowly got to his knees; pushing forward, he managed with her help to get most of his long body up on the mattress.

Quickly she pulled off his boots and turned him over. Moving the lamp closer, she saw the chain link bruises oozing blood. "Jesus Christ!" she gasped, unbuttoning his shirt.

Pouring water into the basin, she cleaned his face with a wet cloth, then gently dabbed at the oozing tracks of the chain.

"Where . . . ?" Clint murmured.

"My place," she said quietly. "I heard you was in jail."

"Got to git . . ." He struggled to rise and failed.

"You're safe here."

"Got to find . . . the judge . . ."

"It'll wait, Clint," Ruby said. "What happened?"

"Somethin' in my coffee . . . sweet . . . pulled me down . . ."

"Laudanum." Ruby nodded. "I use it myself, but not so much."

"Arbuckle . . . had a chain . . ."

154

"Where is he?" Ruby asked, rinsing out the cloth and laying it over Clint's eyes.

"Dead . . . ," Clint whispered. "Deader'n hell."

"He was trash," Ruby said. "Your head'll clear up pretty soon, but you might have a busted collarbone."

"Got to git . . . find the judge . . ." Clint lapsed into a borderline narcosis, and Ruby loosened his belt, unbuttoned his jeans, and covered him with a blanket.

Sitting on the edge of the bed, she tried to think of some way to help the tall, cheerful cowboy who had stood up for her only a few days before.

Clint's breath rattled deep in his chest. His oozing bruises crusted over, and the terrible aching pain racking his body drifted away.

"That's it, Clint, get some rest. I'll watch."

Ruby leaned over, kissed his forehead, and settling down alongside him, stared at the canvas ceiling.

Got to hide him or get him out of town before daybreak. He's too beat up to ride.

In the morning, the sheriff would be sure to swear in a batch of townspeople and start searching for Clint.

Crib row, set off by itself in the alley behind the Buffalo Saloon and Oberlin's Livery, was too simply built to hide much of anything, she thought.

She couldn't ask for help from anybody in the saloon, because she didn't trust the gamblers, fancy dandies, or even Dill Fogarty, the old buffalo hunter who owned the place and rented out cribs as well. Everybody in that saloon was looking for some way to live without working, and lawmen paid for their information.

Maybe Norah Kitt next door would help. She was fair and square, but sick a lot now. One of these days, Dill Fogarty would kick her out for not making the rent, then it'd be the scrub bucket for her until she coughed her lungs up.

She felt Clint's body tremble in his sleep and a painful mumbling coming from his swollen lips, and she pressed against him as if she could give him the strength she had to spare until the spasmodic shaking passed by.

Clint had his gunbelt, but he'd never be able to put up a fight with a gun or anything else until his system was cleansed of the opium tincture and the pain-raddled nerves repaired.

Time. He needed time to rebuild. At least a day.

Have to be a place where she could tend him.

She wondered if the new young doctor would help, maybe put him in the cot in his office and check him over for broken bones.

No, she decided, young Doctor Snordt was different from the old-time medicos she'd known. This one charged a lot of money for his pills, and he demanded cash, no matter who it was. His prices stuck because he was the only doc in town. None of the girls in the row would go to him anymore, because not only did Snordt charge double for an examination, he enjoyed himself so much, they figured he ought to be the one payin'.

The judge? She didn't know Judge Chamberlain, but she'd serviced a few judges here and there, and they didn't behave any different from anyone else once they got their pants off.

No, she had to keep Clint here and let nobody know except maybe Norah Kitt. It was going to be damn near impossible.

There was an open lean-to tacked onto the back of each crib where you could store a trunk if there was room left among the accumulated trash, but anybody searching could clear out the stuff in a couple minutes.

Her trunk wasn't big enough to hold him, anyway.

Again a wave of pain rippled through Clint's

protesting body, and she laid her arm over his bare chest and held him tight until it faded away.

Couldn't hide him in the outhouse, because they'd look there for sure. Couldn't drag him up to the schoolhouse for the same reason. Couldn't get him into the haymow of the livery because he was too big, and old Oberlin just might be drunk and belligerent because he was some cozy with Arbuckle.

Her thoughts kept coming back to the lean-to. Quickly getting up from the bed, she carried the lamp out the flimsy back door.

There was her trunk, and a brass boiler that somebody used for target practice. There was a broken chair and the remains of a clock. There was a cracked ten-gallon salt-glazed crock, a set of harness hames, and a couple empty kegs that had once held horseshoes. There was a pile of discarded curtain material, a crate of empty whiskey bottles, a rotting saddle, a couple of hickory-spoked wagon wheels, and there at the side of the lean-to was an old iron-bound wooden water trough that had sat too long, empty in the sun.

She touched the gray, weathered wood and nodded.

Maybe with Norah's help, they could do it.

Clint stirred when she returned a couple

of hours later, and mumbled, "Drink of water?"

"Right here, Clint." Ruby gave him an enameled dipper half full and put it to his lips.

Seeing her leaning over him, he said slowly, "Thanks, Ruby. How long have I been out?"

"Couple hours," Ruby replied quietly. "You needed the time, and more too."

"Got to git," Clint said, struggling to rise.

"Can you eat?" Ruby asked.

Clint shook his head. "My jaws feel like they're riveted together."

"Head all right?"

"From the laudanum? I better get up and see."

"Come on, cowboy, I'll give you a hand."

Putting Clint's left arm around her shoulders, she let him gather his strength and said, "Ready?"

"Ready as ever," he muttered, and with her lifting, he made it up on wobbly legs.

"Walk out back," she said. "Get you limbered up some."

"My gun?" Clint felt vainly for his revolver.

"I've got it."

She helped him to the back door and awkwardly eased him through it sideways.

She and Norah had worked at cleaning up the lean-to area, and now in the lamplight it looked like a small sun parlor.

The broken chair sat by an upside-down nail keg that was covered with cloth so it resembled a table. A chipped china vase sat on the cloth, and in the vase were three tired ostrich feathers. Much of the other worthless junk had been piled outside, and the water trough had been dragged up close to the back of the crib. It lay upside down and, with a length of tapestry curtain material covering it, resembled a bench.

In front of the trough the big crock had been upended and covered with a cloth so that it too served as a table upon which Ruby had placed her sewing kit and a pile of her beribboned bloomers and lacy unmentionables.

Looking over the lean-to, Clint put away the pain that arrived as his muscles stretched. He still couldn't take a deep breath without the knifing jab in his lungs, but his head was clear at last and he could hardly believe his ragged remembrance of fighting Arbuckle for the chain.

Still, it had happened. He could see the welts of the links across his shoulder. The collarbone was bruised badly but not broken, and he said, "I can't stay here, Ruby."

"Where would you go?"

"Find the judge. I can't wait for him to show up."

"You don't know where he is. You're in

160

no shape to travel."

"He'll be up at Miles City, likely," Clint said thoughtfully.

"You'll never make it. They'll catch you first."

Her words were interrupted by the sound of a shot fired from across the gulch and men yelling, "Wake up! All hell's broke loose!"

"You see?" Ruby asked calmly. "We've been lucky to have this long. Day's breaking."

She blew out the lamp and set it on the inverted crock along with the mending, and asked, "Trust me, Clint?"

"Get Doc! Get everybody!" Sheriff Cox charged out of the jail and sounded the alarm.

Cox holstered his six-gun and paced up and down in front of his office, while skinny Lafe Nofziger, odd-jobs man, who had been poking around early, hoping to find something worth carrying away, ran to get Doc Snordt.

"The goddamned son of a bitch!" Cox was still half drunk from a long night at the Queen playing monte and nursing a bottle of Montana whiskey. He wasn't sure if he was madder at Clint for breaking jail or at his deputy for being stupid enough to go into that cell with a chain.

He'd known about the chain and the way Arbuckle liked to play with it, making it snake around chair legs or strike at stray dogs, and he'd heard the story of the horse Arbuckle had beat to death, but he'd never thought the damned fool would try to use it on a prisoner.

It wasn't remorse for Arbuckle that bothered Cox, it was losing the prisoner he valued as a hefty lifetime pension.

Striding back into the jail, he saw the bloody boot prints and a smear on the wall where Durby had lurched against it, and another on down.

Arbuckle must have half killed him before the tables turned.

Hardly glancing at the purple-faced, bulging-eyed Arbuckle, he prodded the boy with his boot. Almost stiff. Dead five or six hours. A big head start.

Back in the office he noticed Clint's gunbelt was gone, and a bloody palm mark near the peg where he'd leaned a moment.

He's armed, Cox thought, but he's hurt too. Maybe that's worse, like chasing a wounded grizzly bear.

Lafe Nofziger's cries aroused several citizens, including young Doctor Snordt.

"What's the trouble, Sheriff?" Doc Snordt asked sleepily.

"Better look at Arbuckle inside."

"Who's paying?" Snordt asked without moving.

"What the hell? Do you charge for looking at a dead man?" the sheriff yelled, his nerves raw from the past night. "Get in there."

"I'll look, that's all," Snordt said quickly and hustled inside.

"You'll get that chain off him or I'll lock you up!"

Holstein, the mercantiler, arrived, shoving his shirttails in his pants, as well as Sy Haavik, the barber, Asa Ewing, the harness maker, and even old Ike Armsbury, pegging along with others in the distance.

Dan Oberlin came trotting up from the gulch, and Cox demanded, "Did Durby take one of your horses last night?"

"Hell, no, Sheriff," Oberlin replied hotly. "And you don't need to yell at me, either."

"He had his own horse," Lafe Nofziger put in.

"No, Curly and Shorty took that horse back to the Sawtooth," Cox growled. "They was goin' to put it in Oberlin's barn, but I said there was no use in it, as we'd be hangin' Durby."

"So, he's afoot?" Holstein asked in his thick German accent.

"I'd say so." The sheriff turned to the beanpole Nofziger. "I'm deputizing you to replace Arbuckle, and I'm deputizing everybody else temporary. We're goin' to search this

163

damn town from end to end."

"What's Doc doin' in there?" Asa Ewing asked suspiciously, peering in the open door.

"Arranging the body. You can look later," the sheriff muttered. "We'll start at the west end and search every damn house in town."

Taking a dozen men, Cox commenced the search.

"Look out for blood!" Cox yelled at the men. "He's got it all over the jail."

Despite the failing enthusiasm of the searchers and the indignant protests of female householders, Cox held to his plan but found no trace of the fugitive.

"Keep a-moving! He'll be across the gulch, and watch out, he's got a gun!"

"Hell's afire, Sheriff," Deputy Nofziger said, "I ain't got a gun —"

"If you see him, yell, that's all. You don't need to try anything foolish."

"He's not in my barn," Oberlin said. "I'da heard him."

"You were so drunk last night he could have stole the whole barn and you wouldn't have known it," Cox growled. "We'll look through it."

Three men climbed warily into the haymow and pitchforked loose hay from one corner to another, driving the sharp tines into suspicious-looking clumps, while the others poked through the stalls and grain barrels.

Minutes later they met in front of the Buffalo Saloon, an old one-story log building that had once served as a warehouse for green buffalo hides.

"Dill Fogarty ain't goin' to like us comin' in there less'n we buy somethin'," Lafe Nofziger said, licking his dry lips.

"Not a drink till we find that son of a bitch," Cox growled.

They trooped into the dirt-floored, odoriferous saloon, and Cox hammered on the bar. "Dill! Dill Fogarty!"

"Good Christ! Can't a man ever get any sleep?"

In a moment a squat, broad-shouldered, stubble-faced man entered from a back room, squinted at the crowd, and said, "Now what?"

"Durby's broke jail. We're searchin' the whole town," Cox said.

"Fine, search all day. Just don't look in the bottles." Dill Fogarty glared at the men, and turned back to his room.

Cox followed him and saw a canvas cot with a rumpled blanket. Odds and ends of clothing hung from pegs in the log walls, but there was no other furniture and no place for a grown man to hide.

"Damn it," Cox said, coming out into the

main room, "we'll have to go through the cribs."

"There might be somebody else in there," Nofziger said nervously, his Adam's apple bobbing up and down.

"You mean like Banker Rowan?" Oberlin sniggered.

"Or maybe some salty cowboy don't want to be disturbed," Asa Ewing put in.

"Hell, there's only three of 'em," Cox growled, and led the way into the back alley, which looked a good deal more tidy than he remembered.

Knocking at the first door, he yelled, "Open up!"

After a moment a harsh, gravelly voice came back. "I'm closed till five o'clock."

"It's me, Maybelle," the sheriff said persistently, and in a moment the door was opened by a huge woman dressed in a man's nightshirt, adjusting a henna-colored wig on her head.

"We're searchin' the premises," the sheriff said. "Anybody in there?"

"Just Mr. Rowan," she responded bleakly.

"What the hell's going on?" The banker's face, mottled red with anger, appeared in the doorway.

"Sorry to disturb you, sir," Cox said, backing off. "Durby broke jail."

"He's not in here, I promise you that," Banker Rowan snarled and slammed the door.

"Touchy, ain't he?" Nofziger said.

The next two cribs were vacant, silent and empty. At the next door Cox repeated his summons: "Open up!"

"Come on in," came the voice of Norah Kitt. "I'm out with the flowers, but I need the money."

The sheriff, followed by Nofziger, pushed open the door, and saw the sallow-faced Norah Kitt lying in bed.

Nofziger looked under the bed and went out the back door to the cluttered, open lean-to.

"I ain't been well," Norah said weakly. "It just won't quit."

The sheriff's face reddened, embarrassed by what he called female complaints.

"Who's next door?" Cox demanded.

"You know, Ruby Campbell. She's been takin' care of me. Tryin' to buy medicine and such. It's a hard life —"

"You picked it," the sheriff growled, backing out the door.

"I been thinkin' on that," Norah replied seriously, "but seeing how bad things were back home, I really didn't have much choice —"

The sheriff banged his fist on the door of the last crib.

"Come around back," Ruby Campbell called.

Cox led the way around the shanty to the lean-to and saw that it was fixed up as a sort of outdoor sitting room.

Ruby sat on a bench, mending some ruffly thing.

"What a surprise," Ruby cried out, seeing the crowd of men staring at her. "I'd say come into my modest parlor and have a cup of coffee, but I'm afraid there's just not room for you all."

"Look through the crib, Nofziger," Cox growled, and to Ruby, he said quickly, "We're lookin' for a killer. He's close by and damn dangerous."

"That's strong language, Sheriff," she said sharply. "It may not be much, but this is my house and I'd appreciate your respecting it."

"Sorry, ma'am," the sheriff said, taking off his hat. "I've been havin' a hard time. That joker Durby killed my deputy and broke jail last night."

"He could have ridden a good many miles by now," she said.

"He couldn't. I sent his horse out to the ranch and there ain't none been stole."

"Likely he's walkin', then."

168

Ruby gathered up a pile of intimate underthings from beside her and put them on the round crock table. "Would you care to sit down?"

The sheriff blushed and backed off. "No, thanks."

Nofziger came out the door and said, "Clean as a pin."

"If Durby turns up, give a yell," the sheriff said, anxious to be gone.

"Certainly, Sheriff," Ruby Campbell said, inspecting a scanty white lace item with frilly ribbons and bows of pink, holding it up to the light and shaking her head.

"I don't know how this got into my mending — I can't see anything wrong with it, can you, Sheriff?"

"No'm," the lean old gunfighter said, his face bright red, his voice strangled. Cox turned on his heel and, followed by the grinning posse, headed uptown.

# CHAPTER 10

Pulling the tapestry off the old water trough, Ruby spoke softly. "They're gone, Clint. You still alive?"

Clint answered by pushing up on the edge of the trough and levering it over.

"You're lookin' a little less like an oozy corpse and more like a human being," Ruby said, looking him up and down.

"I owe you more than thanks," Clint said.

"Hell, I haven't had so much fun since the hogs ate the twins." Ruby laughed. "That sheriff thinks killin' people makes him into a he-man, but it don't."

"I heard that about my horse," Clint said, walking a short circle to loosen up his legs. "I've got to have him back."

"You can't," Ruby said. "They took him out to Sawtooth."

"I got to have him," Clint said steadily. "Where did the sheriff and his busybodies go?"

"Likely back to the Calico Queen."

"Oberlin too?"

"He's never missed out on a free drink in

his life." Ruby nodded. "You thinkin' of stealin' a horse on top of everything else?"

"Yes'm," Clint said, unsmiling.

"Good luck, cowboy," she said softly as he walked around the side of the crib, crossed the alley, and slipped through the back door of the livery barn.

Pausing at the door, Clint listened for voices, then eased into the shadows of the barn. Motes of dust hung in light shafts coming through cracks in the wall, and horses' hooves thudded restlessly against the dirt floor. Sparrows flitted in and out the double front door, and a pinto cat slept in a feed box, safe from prowling dogs.

No sound of anyone, friendly or hostile.

Clint walked down the alleyway between the stalls: a team of heavy-muscled draft horses, a hammer-headed mustang, a gray, big-shouldered mule, a pair of black coach horses, a roan stud that threw a hind hoof at him as he passed, a heavy-bellied mare ready to foal, an ordinary-looking sorrel gelding with white scar patches on his hindquarters, a steeldust quarter horse that had to belong to either the doctor or the lawyer.

He didn't look any further.

Softly talking horse nonsense in a low voice, he took the blanket that covered a black-tooled leather saddle, spread it over the steeldust's powerful back, and followed it with the saddle and matching bridle.

Backing the steeldust out of the stall, Clint thought, I never stole a horse before, but there's laws and then there's laws.

Outside in the alley, keeping his eyes on the steeldust's hindquarters in case he was a kicker, Clint grabbed the horn and, in one swift flowing motion, was in the saddle, ready for all hell to break loose from the strange horse.

Nothing. The steeldust waited for guidance, his head up and alert, glad to be out of the barn and anxious to run.

Kneeing the steeldust forward, Clint felt power flow through the animal. He held him at a slow trot as he pointed him eastward past the few scanty shacks at the edge of town, but once clear, he turned left off the wagon trace and headed for the timber.

Keeping to the edge of the timber, he rode an arc around the town and in half an hour cut the western wagon trace that would lead to Sawtooth Ranch.

Here he let the steeldust stretch his legs in an easy, smooth canter that ate up the miles without forcing the horse to waste his energy.

The smooth, three-beat gait allowed his body to get reorganized, abraded muscles to heal, skewed joints to come into line, blood to feed the injured tissues and carry off the toxic poisons. With every mile he felt more like his old self, but the ride did little to bring back his old smile.

Thinking on it, he wondered what judgment would be passed on the three bigwigs. Would they hang?

With fast-talking lawyers, likely they'd only get prison terms. Maybe thirty years apiece, enough time that they'd never go free again.

Send 'em down to the federal pen in Laramie and let 'em remember how much fun it was to hunt down the kid and kill him. . . .

*You'd be the best cattleman in Montana Territory if you'd ever grow up. . . .*

"I'm tryin', Lee, I'm tryin' . . . ," he murmured.

Old Judge Chamberlain had hanged a lot of bad men around the Territory. Tim Corn for bushwhackin' . . . Whitey Liggett for rustlin' . . . Sam Rudebaugh for leavin' his sportin' gal to freeze in a snowbank . . . Cisco Ramirez for killin' a guard . . . Lefty Page for changin' brands . . . Big Nose Kelly for knifin' a soldier . . . Candy Clark for borrowin' the wrong horse . . . Hell of a lot of stretched necks. 'Course, none of 'em had two dimes to rub together, but then big money was never caught doin' murder before — leastwise, not that anybody ever heard of.

173

There was something troubling in that list of hanged men, and he knew it was because each one of them had been born poor and died poor.

How did that Mexican song go . . . ? "La Vida No Vale Nada" . . .

Life has no value, life is worth nothing.
We are born with crying and die with
    crying
For that reason, in this world life has no
    value.

He wondered if the Duke of Dorset had any thoughts along that line or Senator Cooley or Big Jim Ralston. . . . Likely not. Too busy figuring how to cheat the poor folks and Indians and Mexicans. Too busy bribin' public officials and grabbin' up public land to think along those lines.

He wondered what they thought about when they took time off from business. Buyin' a new suit of clothes? Lookin' for a younger, fresher woman? Which wine to drink with their broiled salmon? Whether to build another wing on the new mansion? What size diamond ring to buy and how many?

Likely that'd be it, assumin' they ever took time off from schemin' new thievin'.

But there was always that question nagging

in the back of his mind: Where was the justice in hanging just poor folks? Were the rich too powerful to hang?

As he neared the ranch headquarters, he reined the steeldust off the trace and brought him down to an easy trot.

Time to put your mind on how to get that saddle back without gettin' yourself killed doin' it . . . and that ain't goin' to be easy in the middle of the day.

Staying on the sidehill in the big timber, he rode an arc that put him on a slope where he could look down at the big lodge, the bare yard, the barn, corrals, sheds, cookhouse, and bunkhouse, all the ranchstead backed up to the shelter of the mountain.

Where will they put the casino? he wondered. Where will the racecourse be? The fancy hotel all painted pink and white with a black servant in uniform for every room? Where will the railroad depot go? Out of sight, likely. Where will they hide the sporting girls and all the hired help? God knows, they'll have enough land to do it any way they want.

He saw men move back and forth in the yard, so distant they looked like ants. He thought he saw his bay gelding in the corral, and he concentrated his attention on the tack shed where Shorty or Curly would have hung his old saddle.

Judge will only stay in town tomorrow. He'll be off for Virginia City or Billings the next day. Got to time it just right or them rascals will skedaddle out of my range. . . .

"You ready for a run, steeldusty?" he murmured to the impatient horse, who was ready to go another twenty miles full out.

Looking down the slope, he saw that he could gain some cover if he came down behind the long bunkhouse, make a short dash to the tack shed, grab his saddle, then ride like hell back the same way he'd come.

Dang it, I hope there ain't any brave boys down there anxious to shoot me, he thought, his right hand loosening the Colt .44 on his hip. It ain't that I'm meanin' to steal anything. . . .

Riding down in long switchbacks, sometimes letting the big horse slide directly down on his heels and haunches, Clint came out of the trees behind the bunkhouse, which had only two small windows on the blind side.

Walking the steeldust quietly to the edge of the building, he held there a moment, turned the corner, and walked the horse more into the open, his eyes alert for any motion.

With any luck, they'd be out chasin' strays or moving cattle and only Cooky would be working in his kitchen.

The overhead sun beat down onto the bare

yard, and Clint pulled his wide hatbrim down to shade his eyes from the glare. At the last second he decided to walk the horse over to the shed instead of making an unnatural flurry that would only attract attention.

Out in the bare sunlit yard, his nerves tightened up and screamed at him to hurry, but he held the steeldust to a steady walk toward the tack shed, trying to look like he belonged there.

He caught a movement out of the corner of his eye and saw far over on the veranda of the lodge a small man in a gray frock coat coming out the door.

Plenty of time, he told his worried mind with little confidence and held to the walk.

Reaching the corner of the shed, he turned the steeldust to the right and swung down in front of the open door.

There was his saddle forking a peeled log along with a couple others. All he had to do was take three steps, grab its horn, and go out the same way he'd come in.

Only thing, old Badger Corbin was at the bench, rubbing beeswax into his six-gun holster, and the worn Colt was lying there right by his hand.

" 'Lo, Badger," Clint said, going into the shed. "I come for my saddle."

"That all?" Badger asked, his hand moving

quickly to the Colt, holding it pointed at Clint's chest.

"Didn't come to shoot with you or anyone else," Clint said. "I'm plumb peaceable."

"How'd you get out of jail?" Badger asked, holding the Colt steady.

"They decided it was all a mistake," Clint said easily. "Now, if you'll just put that smoke pole down, I'll be on my way."

"They'd never let you out," Badger said, his old agate eyes watching Clint carefully. "Step back, and drop your gunbelt."

"Look, Badger, I don't have time to argue. Just let me take my saddle and that'll be the last of it."

"I'm countin' to three. One."

Clint could think of no trick that would upset Badger enough to miss, yet he couldn't allow himself to be taken prisoner again. "Two."

Clint took a deep breath, unclasped the buckle, and the gunbelt and holstered six-gun fell to the floor.

"Hold it right there!" came the voice of Senator Cooley standing at the door, a two-bore twelve-gauge crooked in his arm, and aimed directly at Clint's back.

"I'm willin'," Clint replied quickly, raising his hands, turning a quarter circle to keep both men in view.

"You in there, Badger?" the senator crowed.

"I got him under my gun, Senator," Badger replied stolidly.

"Fine!" The senator smiled, lowering his shotgun. "Now, let's have a little talk."

"Go ahead," Badger said sourly. "I'm done talkin'."

"What brought you back out here?" The gray-suited popinjay beamed. "Homesick?"

"Something like that, Senator. I just stopped by on my way to California to pay my respects," Clint drawled.

"With such an aptitude for lying, you should have gone into politics." The senator chuckled. "Now, what about the truth, for a change?"

"What have you done with Emily Smith?" Clint asked directly.

"Sweet on her, Durby?" The senator's eyes glittered. "She's locked up downstairs. Soon as we go east, she goes west."

"She didn't steal nothin'," Clint said. "She don't deserve to be punished."

"I was finished with her anyway, Durby," the senator said. "Where she's going, she just might learn to enjoy herself instead of whining all the time."

"Why not just let her go her own way? It's a free country."

"Durby, quit wasting my time. Why are you here?" The senator lifted the shotgun an inch.

"I figured to pick up my bedroll and war bag," Clint said. "It's goin' to be a long trip."

"That ain't true neither," Badger growled. "You come for your saddle."

"It's a good old saddle. Fits my head all night same as it fits my butt all day," Clint said, patting the hard, shiny seat, letting his hand settle on the latigo-wrapped horn.

"Likely you told my man Mikowski some kind of mush like that just before you killed him," the senator said, and took a step forward.

"Don't get too close to him, Senator. The son of a bitch is quicker'n a cat with his tail afire," Badger warned.

"He's not as quick as my trigger finger." The senator smiled. "I'm rather hoping he'll try me."

"Senator, I don't never argue with a greener. It makes a sorry corpse," Clint drawled.

Badger had not relaxed for an instant, and though the senator had lowered the shotgun barrel and was enjoying the cat-and-mouse game, he had only to lift it six inches and pull the triggers to cut Clint in half at the waistband.

Clint was ready to shake his head in futility and make a desperate leap for the twelve-gauge when Badger said, "My arm's got a kink in it, Senator. Can you keep him covered?"

"Delighted," the senator said. "I haven't had so much fun in years."

"Kick that gunbelt over this way, Durby," Badger said, not holstering his Colt but letting it just hang down to his side as his arthritic elbow demanded.

"Sure thing, Badger," Clint said pleasantly. "Don't get nervous now, Senator. You heard what the man said."

"Go ahead, kick it over." Cooley nodded toward the gun.

Clint turned toward Badger with exaggerated slowness, as if he were afraid any sudden move might make the senator touch the triggers.

"Easy does it," Clint said.

His boot toe touched the gunbelt and his right hand gripped the saddle horn, then with a long sigh he sent the full force of his leg muscles into kicking the six-gun and belt directly up into Badger Corbin's face. At the same time he flung the saddle at the shotgun.

Without hesitating, he leaped away from the door toward Badger as the shotgun fired. Badger pawed the gunbelt away and brought his six-gun up as Clint grabbed at it with his left hand and brought his right hand across too late.

The Colt roared as Clint tried to force it out of Badger's grip, and he felt a burning pain in his left leg.

Bringing his right elbow across into Badger's weather-hardened face, he swung Badger's arm down toward the floor with his left hand and wrenched the six-gun free. Badger's right hand chased after the six-gun, grabbed it by the barrel, and tried to force the muzzle toward the shed roof.

He hadn't the strength of Clint, and midway, the Colt belched lead and flame again; the bullet smacked through Badger's right shoulder, driving him back against the workbench.

Quickly, Clint shifted the Colt to his right hand to meet the senator's charge.

It didn't come, and Clint realized the cowardly senator was too afraid to come help Badger.

"That's your old buddy," Clint growled at Badger, who was backing away, his left hand cradling his right elbow.

Grabbing his gunbelt, Clint jammed Badger's six-gun in his waistband and pulled out his own fully loaded .44.

"You son of a bitch," Badger said, breathing heavily, his eyes loaded with hatred.

"Count your blessings you didn't kill yourself," Clint said, feeling the pain bite into his leg.

He could walk on it — the bone wasn't broken, the artery was intact — but somewhere out there was a little man with a big shotgun. Maybe he had one round left or maybe he had a pocketful.

"Move out there," Clint ordered the older man, who didn't seem to hear.

"I said move out the door!" Clint stepped close to Badger in a fury, and pulled him away from the bench into the open doorway.

There was no report from the shotgun, and Clint had to guess whether the senator had run for help or was playing a waiting game.

Either way, there was no time.

So, if he's smart, he'll be off to the right, behind the feed trough, cutting me off from my horse.

Setting himself a moment, he pictured what he was going to run into, then leaped out the door, whirling and aiming at the same time toward the feed trough.

There was no one there. Instantly he dived to the ground as the shotgun roared off to his left and buckshot tore at his hat.

Rolling to the right, he saw the little man at the corner of the shed break open the shotgun and feed two more brass-cased loads into the tubes.

Badger was gone.

Clint's first snap shot drove splinters off the shed, but by now the shotgun was loaded. The senator raised it to fire point-blank, a victorious smile on his cherubic lips.

Clint's second desperate shot took the senator in the leg, dropping him to his knees; as the senator labored to touch the triggers, Clint's fourth slug smacked him in the high paunch, driving him over backward. The shotgun fired into the air, and as Clint grabbed his slug-riddled saddle, the senator rolled toward him, both hands holding his bulging abdomen. "Help me . . . ," Cooley groaned, bloody froth bubbling on his lips. "Help me . . . I'll help you . . ."

"No deals today, Senator . . . ," Clint murmured, hobbling toward the steeldust.

Figures appeared on the veranda of the lodge, and around to his right, Cooky was standing in the cookhouse doorway, both hands held high.

Clint snapped a shot toward the veranda to check the oncoming bodyguards as he reached the steeldust's near side.

Got to do it, leg, he thought, and fitted his

bloody boot into the stirrup, gripped the horn. With a little groan breaking out of his rigid jaw, he put his weight on the leg and swung aboard.

Turning the steeldust, he leaned down to grab the horn of his saddle on the ground, when a bullet screamed over his head.

Not hesitating, he settled his old saddle on his lap and rode for the cover of the tack shed, where the Right Honorable Senator Lorenzo Cooley lay in the dust.

Clint set the steeldust into a run around the back side of the tack shed, and as firing erupted from the lodge, the steeldust leaped across the open space with powerful strides that took them into the protection of the timber. Clint eased off and let the great animal pick his way through the pines as he climbed the slope and turned easterly.

Coming to a secluded, ferny glen, Clint halted the horse, painfully dismounted, and pried off his bloody boot.

As he'd suspected, the trajectory of the bullet had been downward and had nicked his calf but hadn't gone through.

Wrapping his bandanna around the wound, he looked at his ruined saddle, worried off the leather rosette with his teeth, and slid the green notebook out of its hiding place.

Opening it to the last entry, he read, "It's

going to be hard to stop these pirates . . . wish big brother was here to help out."

Wasn't there to help out, Clint thought sadly. Was in jail for playin' the fool.

# CHAPTER 11

The next day Judge Gibbon Chamberlain arrived in town and turned the schoolhouse into a makeshift courtroom. Located on the west side of town as far away from nauchtown as it could be placed, the schoolhouse was a squat, no-nonsense brick structure divided into two rooms plus an office for the teacher. Its front door opened into a cloakroom. The back door led from the teacher's office to the backyard, empty except for a four-hole privy. A few bedraggled aspens and pines, worn out by young climbers and swingers, lined the path.

At nine in the morning Judge Chamberlain, seated at the teacher's desk with his young assistant at a table close by, took the turned walnut gavel from his traveling bag and banged it three times on the desk.

Chamberlain, a thin man of average height, but with a sense of personal presence that seemed to add another half a foot to his stature, looked quickly around the room with sharp, piercing eyes.

A luminous glow emanated from his porcelain-white face, freshly shaven, steamed and powdered by Sy Haavik only minutes before. Separating his deep-set hawk eyes was a long thin nose, the bony bridge a catenary arch that came level with his thin colorless upper lip. It was a hard New England face untempered by mercy but dedicated to dispensing justice quickly and efficiently, and it was haloed by a corona of long, fine white hair.

Judge Chamberlain prided himself on his ability to get to the bottom of any case in a matter of minutes, the sooner the better.

His clerk served as a general amanuensis as well as coach driver and errand boy. For this he received little money, but in a couple more years he would have learned how to foment litigation and would go out on his own to seek his fortune.

"All rise!" the clerk called out.

As the few onlookers stood, the young man ran through his preamble in an incoherent blur, "First-Circuit-Court-of-Montana-Territory-now-in-session-be-seated . . ."

With a scuffling of chairs and school benches, the audience sat down again.

"First-case-people-against-Carmody-Andrews . . . charged-with-attempted-stagecoach-robbery —"

"Prisoner rise." Judge Chamberlain pointed his gavel at a short, bowlegged cowboy wearing a scuffed leather vest, a worn shirt, and jeans.

"How do you plead?" the judge asked in a resonant voice, his hawk eyes fixed on the cowboy.

"Judge, I was drunk . . . ," the cowboy said, looking at the oiled pine floor.

"Mr. Andrews, you must plead guilty or innocent," the judge said patiently. "How do you plead, sir?"

"Guilty, I reckon."

"Very well, Mr. Andrews pleads guilty to the charge. Now please briefly tell the court any extenuating circumstances." The judge nodded to the small man, encouraging him to speak up.

"I was drinkin' and I run out of money," the short puncher said. "I got the stage stopped, and the driver threw down the strongbox, but when I leaned down from my pony to pick it up, I was so drunk I fell off and the damn — beg pardon, Judge — the blamed pony run off. I wouldn't have done it if I'd been in my right mind."

"How can the court know whether you would or would not?"

"Well, I never did it before and I sure won't ever try a fool trick like that again," the puncher said, looking at the judge directly.

"I believe you, Carmody Andrews, but you

know the laws concerning highway robbery as well as I do. It is not permitted and it is not encouraged by giving out light sentences. Have you anything else to say?"

"Well . . . I was figurin' on gettin' married and settlin' down, come fall," the puncher said shyly.

"I'm afraid not, Mr. Andrews. The sentence of this court is no more and no less than is usually granted, and that is twenty years in Fort Laramie Prison. Next case."

"Oh, Judge!" Andrews cried out without thinking, but was cut off by the banging of the gavel.

As a tall, mustachioed federal marshal led the downcast cowboy off to his doom, the judge scanned the faces in the audience.

Sheriff Earl Cox sat in the front row, placid as usual but with a certain intent to his manner.

The very back row held the oddest collection of people he'd ever seen in his frontier court. Two of the men were richly dressed and obviously would never appear in this place unless a serious situation justified it. Attending the two gentlemen were two men of lower class, a powerful-looking redhead and a scarred veteran pug who looked like a cold-blooded assassin.

He banged the gavel again and the room

settled down. "Next case."

"Next case, Your Honor," the clerk read from his agenda, "is Sheriff Cox's application for a murder warrant against one Clinton Durby, now a fugitive from justice."

"What's this all about, Sheriff?" the judge asked quietly, his eyes on Cox.

"Durby," the sheriff said, rising and holding his hat over his midriff, "has killed three men, including my deputy and Senator Lorenzo Cooley of Pennsylvania. Durby broke jail, stole a horse, and threatened the lives of the gentlemen in the back row."

"Senator Cooley murdered?" The judge frowned. "I knew him well. We're from the same state. What's behind all this, Sheriff?"

"Well, this puncher, Durby, stole some papers from the main house out on Sawtooth, then killed a man and run for it. I arrested him, but he killed Deputy Arbuckle and escaped. Yesterday he turned up at the ranch on a stolen horse, wounded the ranch foreman, and shot the senator. That's about the size of it, Your Honor."

"Why haven't you apprehended him, Sheriff?"

"I figure if I could get some federal marshals helpin', I could run him down pronto."

"So that's why you want the federal warrant?"

"Yes, Your Honor, we want it to be all legal and proper, so there won't be no scandal attached to the Sawtooth Syndicate."

"It is a very serious accusation, most especially because of the prominence of Senator Cooley," the judge said. "He was highly thought of and a great statesman. His leadership will be missed by the entire nation."

Glancing at the clerk, Judge Chamberlain added, "Draw up the warrant."

"Yes, Your Honor," the clerk said, taking a document from his travel case and filling in the blanks.

"Sheriff, put Durby's description on the telegraph wire. I'll have an army of marshals converging on Sawtooth in a matter of hours."

"Thanks, Judge," Sheriff Cox said, sitting down again.

"Now, would you gentlemen please step forward and address the court?" The judge pointed his gavel at the men in the back row.

Clint had ridden to the western edge of town before daybreak and found a secluded hideaway in a grove of alders by the river, where he picketed the steeldust and made his way to the empty schoolhouse.

Entering the teacher's office as the sun rose, he snapped the cast-iron latch on the door leading into the classroom so that he wouldn't be surprised as he waited.

He carried the notebook under his shirt. Badger Corbin's six-gun rode in his waistband next to his backbone, his own .44 was loaded, and he was ready and anxious for justice.

Now it was just keeping awake and waiting.

He wondered what would happen after he gave the book to the judge, but there were just too many unknown possibilities to nail a plan down hard and fast.

It depended on how many bought-out lawmen were there. Depended on whether the main crew of Sawtooth cowboys had returned from their roundup. Depended on who all turned up in the front room in the next couple of hours.

Better to play whatever cards you're dealt as best you can, he thought. For sure, once the judge reads that memorandum those three signed and hears how they killed Lee, he'll lock 'em up.

*You'd make the best cattleman in Montana if you'd just grow up. . . .*

Sorry, little brother, but all the decent range in this Territory has already been hogged down by Swan, Prairie Land Company, Powder River, Union Cattle Company, Sawtooth. . . . Them million-dollar syndicates, they done grabbed all the land with water.

Maybe there's room left out in Nevada for

a small rancher . . .

One thing at a time, he thought tiredly. First we see the judge and get those scalawags behind bars, then we can start working out what comes next.

He heard boots tramp in from the front door, chairs and tables being moved into position, and he stood with the six-gun in his hand as someone tried the office door.

"Schoolmarm got it locked," a voice said on the other side of the door.

"It's not important. There's not much on the docket this morning. We'll be out of here in an hour —"

Clint wondered if it was the judge speaking to his clerk, but there was no way of knowing, so he settled down again to wait until he was damned sure the judge was on the other side of that door.

Not long after, he heard more activity, voices, boot heels, and spurs jingling, then the authority of the gavel announcing that the judge was ready to proceed.

He was all set to go out right then, but the judge didn't waste any time getting into the stagecoach robbery, and he didn't want to make the judge mad by busting into the middle of the case.

Twenty years, in terms of a man's short life, seemed hard punishment to Clint, but it was the standard sentence for such a crime, and you could just say, "Too bad for Carmody Andrews, maybe his example will stop somebody else from making the same mistake." What mistake? he wondered. Dumb, knot-headed cowboy can't hold his liquor. . . .

Unsnapping the lock on the door, Clint was ready to step out and hand the book over to the judge when he heard his own name and Sheriff Cox reading off a list of crimes so fearsome, Clint's confidence faltered.

Durby didn't like the judge saying what a fine, upstanding man the senator was, but that was because he didn't know any better.

Once Judge Chamberlain reads the notebook and the memorandum, he'll change his mind plenty quick.

Goin' to set the federal marshals and likely the Cattlemen's Association on me, Clint thought grimly and knew he'd better do something damned sudden or the judge would already have his mind made up.

Drawing his six-gun and taking the book from under his shirt, Clint kneed the door open and stepped out into the classroom.

He saw Ralston, the duke, and their two bodyguards coming toward the judge. They suddenly froze, and he slowly moved his six-gun in a sweep across the room.

"Don't nobody try nothin'," he said strongly. "I don't want anyone hurt. Now, you all with guns on, raise up your hands —"

"Order in the court!" The judge banged the gavel furiously, and turned his chair so that he could see. The clerk on the other side of him turned pale and was looking for an open window.

"Judge, my name's Clint Durby, same man the sheriff has been lyin' about. Before you start listenin' to these gents, I want to give you this notebook. Inside is a paper that shows what kind of low-down skunks they really are. You can see from my brother's notebook that they deliberately murdered him because he found that paper."

"I don't understand . . ." The judge accepted the notebook, his hawk's gaze moving from the four city-dressed men facing him to the tall cowboy with the gun.

"It's all there, Judge. I'd like you to arrest 'em and give 'em a trial and then hang the rotten devils."

"Put down that gun, Durby. I'll allow nothing like this in my court."

"Them gents would like that, Judge, but I'm sorry I can't oblige," Clint said soberly. "I know it ain't proper behavior in a courtroom, but them dudes make their own rules."

"Your brother collected this evidence?" the

judge asked quietly.

"Yes. He was a good kid working through the summer for Sawtooth. He was set to go back to school, but he got wind of the Sawtooth Sporting Club scheme and thought he could write it up for the papers back east."

"And he was killed, you say?"

"Yes, sir. I dug him up a few hours after they buried him. He had three bullet holes in him, the last one was from about an inch away when he wasn't even able to crawl. They had their bodyguards drive him like an animal for sport and the three of them, including the senator, took turns."

"That's hard to believe, Durby," the judge said slowly.

"The evidence is in the grave and in that notebook. You don't need to believe nothin' I say, except that anybody I've had to shoot in the past few days was tryin' to shoot me first."

"An incredible story . . . ," the judge said, rubbing his thin jaw with his thumb, absorbing and sorting out the different parts. "In the two years I've been holding circuit court across this Territory I've heard some strange cases, but this one is by far the strangest."

"It's true, every word of it," Clint said. "Now, I've done my part, you can deal out the justice."

"Just let me read some of this," the judge said, studying the memorandum. After a few moments he nodded and said, "I believe I know what you are talking about now, Mr. Durby, but I won't proceed until you give me that gun."

"When all the rest of them give you their guns," Clint said.

Clint looked the group over and decided the middleweight bodyguard was the most dangerous. He'd have a bulldog pistol next to his left ribs, and he wasn't afraid of anything.

"May we speak, Your Honor?" the duke asked, his voice soft and smooth.

"Please step forward and address the court," the judge replied.

With Big Jim Ralston, the duke moved forward and spoke in his cultured offhand manner. "My friend and partner here is Mr. C. James Ralston of the Chicago-Seattle Railway. I am Percival, Duke of Dorset. Together with the late Senator Cooley, we own the Sawtooth Cattle Syndicate."

"I've heard of it," the judge said, eyeing the pair closely.

"We leave tomorrow for New York, and we need to recover our property, which this rather demented cowhand has stolen."

"You mean this paper?" the judge tapped

the memo with his bony index finger.

"It's rather an . . . important . . . document, as well as the notebook which the unfortunate boy admitted was false as he lay dying from an accidental gunshot wound. He had hoped to use the notebook and stolen memorandum to extort a great deal of money from the company."

"I see . . ." The judge nodded solemnly, his white hair floating light as milkweed. "He didn't understand business, I suppose."

"He was completely inexperienced," the duke said, nodding diffidently, "but he should have known better than to try to bleed our company."

"Just a minute, Judge —" Clint tried to interrupt, but the judge punched his gavel down and said, "Mr. Ralston, sir, what have you got to say about all this?"

"I concur with the duke," Ralston growled. "Did you say you were from Pennsylvania?"

"That's true," the judge said slowly, his eyes fixed on Ralston's. "My father was a Pennsylvania Supreme Court Justice for many years."

"We should talk in private," Ralston said.

"Very well," the judge replied.

"Judge, I'm askin' for justice for my brother, and the Crow Indians too," Clint said, taking a step backward. "I'm trustin' you'll do the job."

"Put down the gun, Durby," the judge said harshly. "I'll see to your safety. That's a promise."

"Judge, there's no way in hell you can guarantee them skunks won't cut me down."

"I'm the judge of that. A court cannot be run like a battlefield. There must be law and order and time to deliberate carefully. Give me that gun."

"I can't, Your Honor. I'm goin' to get clear now, but I'll be hangin' around waitin' to see how these birds are punished."

"You are in contempt of this court," the judge said coldly. "You are jeopardizing your case with this kind of conduct."

"It's the way it is. I trusted these gents before, and now I'd rather trust a washtub full of rattlesnakes," Clint said.

"Clerk, hold these papers as evidence," the judge said, fitting the memorandum back into the notebook and handing it to the clerk.

"Remember, Judge, them papers cost my brother his life," Clint said with a sinking feeling in his gut as he saw the notebook disappear. "Ain't you goin' to do somethin'?"

"You presume to be above the law, Durby," the judge said, glaring at him. "Put down that gun, or face the consequences."

"Arrest them! Put them in jail! Those four! The sheriff too!" Clint cried out, fearing that he'd built himself a house of cards based on the circuit judge's integrity.

"I will do nothing so long as you hold this courtroom hostage." The judge frowned. "If you want justice, you must accept the laws set down for the protection of all."

"No, Judge, I been a fool, but I ain't crazy. The laws you're talkin' about are made by the big bullfrogs so they can eat up the little tadpoles like me. Soon as they drop me, what can you do? I'm the only witness that will testify against 'em."

The judge turned back to the tense audience and said, "I want no shooting. When this man hands over his gun to me, I am guaranteeing his life. Is that understood?"

The diverse group nodded solemnly, but the tension in the room didn't ease.

"All right, Judge, I'm trustin' you to do right," Clint said, stepping forward and laying the Colt on the table.

The judge quickly passed the revolver to his clerk and banged his gavel. "Sheriff Cox, arrest this man and lodge him in jail until such time as the court deems proper for trial."

Grinning, the sheriff stepped forward, but Clint was already moving backward, his right hand behind his back, protesting. "No, Judge, he's one of 'em!"

"Hold it there," Sheriff Cox growled, drawing his six-gun. "I'm arresting you in the name of the law."

Clint saw the sheriff's finger closing down on the trigger and knew full well he had no intention of taking him alive.

Without thinking, Clint whirled close to the judge, drawing Badger's old Peacemaker out of the back of his waistband, and as the sheriff hesitated, Clint snapped a shot that broke Cox's thighbone and hurled him against a school desk.

The judge banged his gavel in rage, but he had lost control of his court.

With Clint facing the bunch from the Sawtooth, the judge swung the gavel at Clint's right elbow, cracking the crazy bone and momentarily paralyzing Clint's hand.

Quickly shifting the six-gun to his left hand, Clint put the barrel against the fleecy white head and said, "Judge, this means you better damn well do your job or I'm takin' you off the payroll. Understand?"

The judge's luminescent face changed to a very pale green as he felt the muzzle of the Colt hard against his skull. "You'll get your justice, Durby, I promise you that."

"That's all I been askin' for all along, Judge," Clint said, sidling away from the judge toward the teacher's office.

Sheriff Cox groaned and, from the clutter of tipped-over desks and benches, moaned, "Help me, somebody . . ."

Someone yelled, "Call the doc!"

No one moved until Clint motioned with his six-gun. "Get a tourniquet on it!"

Tony Douglas, the Cockney bodyguard, was closest, and whipping off his belt, knelt over the sheriff and pulled the tourniquet tight on the upper thigh, murmuring some sort of sympathy.

"It won't hold," he said sharply to Clint. "He's dying — Take a look!"

As Clint stepped forward, Cox lifted his concealed right hand holding the revolver, and Clint shot the sheriff twice in the chest. Then he saw Tony Douglas's hand come free from under his coat with a .36-caliber Colt swinging up.

Douglas grinned, knowing he had Clint beat a mile, pleased with himself, feeling as if he'd just won a tough street fight, and taking his time, he squeezed the trigger. Clint, without time to aim, dropped the hammer and saw the small Colt fling away from Douglas's undamaged hand.

The duke lifted his right arm as if to point his finger at Clint, and Clint let loose his last round as the duke's sleeve gun barked and sent its single .32-caliber bullet over Clint's head while Clint's bullet tore through the duke's drooping earlobe.

"You can't escape, Durby!" the judge barked. "We'll hunt you down like a mad dog!"

Backing through the door, Clint slammed it shut, set the flimsy lock and, hobbling on his bad leg, made it out the back door and into the trees before the cautious manhunters could commence pursuit.

Reaching the horse in its covert by the stream, Clint mounted up and, hesitating a moment, pointed him west.

Crouching over the steeldust's neck, he asked for a burst of speed to get them clear, and the quarter horse leaped forward, taking huge strides, flying like the wind.

After half a mile, Clint reined the steeldust down to an easy canter so he could reload the Colt, and thought miserably, They've got the evidence, they've got the judge, they've got a hundred federal marshals . . . and all Clint Durby's got is a sore leg and a good horse.

# CHAPTER 12

Riding west, keeping to the timber, Clint didn't bother to hide his trail from pursuers.

He had to recover the notebook, but he knew of no one he could trust to use it against the Syndicate.

Ralston and the duke were so rich and powerful they were untouchable by the laws that governed ordinary citizens. They could have their beaters drive a youngster to their shooting stands and then each one take a shot, the last one right in the face.

Got any ideas, little brother? he thought grimly as he rode through the big trees. I'm willin' — I just ain't got enough furniture in the upstairs parlor to see where we go from here.

His thoughts drifted back over the scene in the schoolroom. How he'd tried to talk about right and wrong to the judge. He might as well have been talkin' to a fence post, because once the judge read that memo, he knew right where the hog trough was and didn't want to be late. There was no doubt in Clint's mind that the duke and Big Jim would still have their "talk in private" with the judge and they would cut him into the deal. They could give him the late senator's share.

Where would they talk? Where were the documents?

The bigwigs were going to leave in the morning . . . so they'd have to come back to the ranch. They'd take Emily to Ralston's railroad depot, and they'd ride east while they sent Emily west.

He considered how much time he had before a posse came riding with orders to shoot to kill.

Without Sheriff Cox, they'd be slow to get organized. Nofziger would be cautious. It would take a while to round up a posse, Clint decided and quit worrying about his back trail. Locating Emily shouldn't take long, but after that, what?

Ride on, drift, punch cows, break horses, look for a little grazing land with water and shelter . . .

But he'd always be looking over his shoulder. They'd never let up.

Tell me, little brother, now that I'm about growed up, what do I do and where do I go?

Laws and laws.

Try to help a sportin' girl buy some medicine and get thrown in the hoosegow. Those three snakes shot my kid brother to pieces and nothing happens.

The poor outlaws hang, the rich outlaws go free.

Justice! his mind screamed in baffled frustration. Kill them all!

One thing at a time, Clint, he caught himself. It's too big otherwise. Think of how Lee would do it. Take it a step at a time until there ain't any more steps.

"Any advice, little brother?" he asked out loud, seeing the young, smiling face and wavy yellow hair, the eagerness and enthusiasm.

Something suddenly caught his mind by the coattail and he looked again, the same face, the lightness and purposefulness blended together in the face, and he thought a second about that lightness and purposefulness.

Lee had worked to put himself through school. That showed a sense of purpose.

He'd written down the cowboy yarns and songs and jokes no matter how unprintable they were, and that showed a purpose.

And he'd not been satisfied to just overhear the Big Three discuss their business, he'd raided their inner sanctum and brought out the signed memorandum.

That was about as much purposefulness as most men wanted.

What had he meant to do? He'd meant to

take the evidence to Chicago, write the story, and give it all to a newspaper.

He hadn't thought to take it to a judge, he'd thought only of putting the whole story in a newspaper for the public to see. He'd figured the people had a right to know the truth, and after that, they could do whatever they wanted.

Even if the Syndicate members owned some newspapers, there was bound to be an editor somewhere with as much sense of purpose as the kid's, anxious to expose profiteers' political corruption.

It's too late. You've lost the notebook, he thought bitterly. There's too many of them. They've got the money and power. You're beat, hands down.

You're just too damned billy-goat stubborn to admit it.

Clint, he told himself dead serious, they killed your brother slow. You can't ride away from that, and that's a fact. . . .

# CHAPTER 13

Clint rode northwesterly, making it look like he was headed for Canada and couldn't be caught. He went slowly to save the steeldust's strength for when it might be needed.

Working his way over a granite ridge, he recognized his landmarks, cut to the east, then put the steeldust on a direct line toward the ranch buildings far off in the distance.

From the way the judge had played his cards in the schoolhouse, Clint decided he wouldn't trust that notebook with any clerk who might have ambitions of his own. The notebook would be close to the judge's hand.

From the distant hillside he saw the surrey standing in front of the lodge. The driver must have whipped the team all the way.

Drifting down to a shallow stream, he let the steeldust drink but kept his eyes on the far ranch yard, which appeared to be empty.

With his right hand brushing against the walnut butt of the Colt .44, he urged the steeldust across the clear rippling water, his eyes alert for any action, hostile or otherwise.

Stopping in front of the bunkhouse, he

heard no knocking boot heels or palaverin' inside. Tethering the big horse at the rail, he glanced over at the cookhouse and noticed there was no smoke coming from the stovepipe.

Stepping into the shadowed bunkhouse, he saw a huddled form on Badger's cot, and moved quickly along the wall, ready to draw and fire.

"Badger?"

The grizzled foreman opened his sunken eyes and stared at Clint as if he didn't recall his name or face.

Clint saw the thick bandage on his shoulder, and said, "You all right?"

"I ain't never been all right, Clint," Badger muttered.

"Where's the boys?" Clint kept the open door in sight.

"They quit. I don't know where the hell they went," Badger growled.

"Quit?"

"Said the place was hoo-dooed. I don't know, maybe they figured they was more men than bungholes."

"Cooky?"

"He couldn't go far on that sprung leg. Seein' how there's nobody else around, likely they put him to guardin' that woman."

"How many came back from town?"

"They was six." Badger shook his head with disgust. "The doc was along, lookin' after the duke."

"Doc look at your shoulder?"

"Hell with him," Badger growled. "He wanted twenty dollars cash money before he'd come in the door. Hell, that's half my month's pay for his five minutes."

"Folks generally get well if they leave the medicos out of it," Clint said, trying to calm the angry old foreman.

"You're crazy to come back. There ain't anywhere in the world you can lay your head in peace anymore," Badger said. "I see now you had the right, but you're still crazy."

"Was the judge with 'em, Badger?" Clint asked.

"They was with a white-haired buzzard. I never saw him before."

"That's Judge Chamberlain. I'm goin' to talk with him."

"You'll end up talkin' to the English pug and that Irish bully," Badger said, laying his head back on the pillow. "Good luck."

Clint moved out of the bunkhouse and, with the sun standing off in the west, took advantage of the long shadows to slip an extra cartridge into the empty chamber under the hammer. If there were six hostile hombres in that lodge, he just might need all six rounds.

Could he safely cross the next fifty yards of hard-baked yard to the lodge?

We will try, do or die, Clint thought, and walked slowly out into the open, knowing if someone happened to glance out the front window, they'd pot him like a turkey tied to a stump.

Eyes moving, scanning the front of the lodge and the trees on either side, he bore left, forcing himself to stroll along, although all his interior warning signals were crying out for him to duck and run.

Coming to the left corner of the veranda, he moved toward the side door that led down to the basement storerooms.

Somewhere along that hallway a guard would be posted.

Goin' to have it out, but it'd better be damn quiet or they'll have you boxed in. . . .

Silently opening the door, he went down the steps, six-gun in hand, ready.

In the dimly lighted hall he saw a figure rising from a chair.

"Cooky?"

"It's me. Don't shoot," Cooky came back quickly.

"Easy does it," Clint said quietly, coming up close and eyeing the chunky belly-robber, stiff right leg sprung out of line, hands up and open.

212

"You're outnumbered, Clint," Cooky said, lowering his hands. "They're all upstairs ready for bear."

"You?"

"I don't hold with gunfightin'." Cooky shook his head. "Once my leg went, I changed my life."

"The lady?"

"Inside." Cooky hooked his thumb at the barred door.

"No point in keepin' her locked up, now that I'm here," Clint murmured, his gaze fixed on Cooky's pasty features. "You goin' to help us?"

"I heard what happened in the schoolhouse, and I ain't about to argue with a crazy man," Cooky said, lifting the bar and pushing the door open.

Dark-haired Emily Smith came to the doorway, the left side of her face swollen and bruised, her eyes haggard.

"Clint," she said, her eyes widening as she recognized him. "You should never have come back."

"My business ain't finished," Clint said. "Cooky will saddle you a horse, then if I don't show up pronto, you ride out fast."

"Clint" — she stared up into his hard eyes — "I want to help."

"Then git goin'." He smiled. "Once you're

in town, tell old pegleg Armsbury at the cafe I sent you to him for safekeeping."

"I'll wait there for you," she said and, standing on her toes, kissed his cheek. She went up the hall with Cooky swinging awkwardly behind her.

She turned at the top of the steps and held up her left hand as if she could prolong the moment.

"Go on," he said softly.

Dropping her hand, she turned and went out the door with Cooky behind her.

Following along, Clint stood at the doorway, watching.

She was halfway across the yard when a heavy hunting rifle boomed from the veranda and dust kicked up in front of her.

Cooky looked fearfully over his shoulder and hopped off to the right, heading for the trees, leaving her caught between the lodge and the corral.

The rifle roared and the heavy slug caught Cooky high between the shoulders, driving him spread-eagled into the dirt.

Emily tried another step and was halted by a rifle bullet raising dust immediately in front of her.

Even as Clint ran alongside the lodge, she turned to look at the veranda where the sporting gentlemen waited.

"Come back," Ralston commanded, holding the sights of his Big Fifty on her bosom, "or I'll kill you."

Clint tried to see a target, but the shooters were too far back on the veranda.

Emily paused a second, careful not to look at Clint crouched at the corner of the veranda.

As she climbed the steps to the veranda, Clint heard Ralston's deep, gravelly voice: "If you try to run off again there'll be no warning shot . . . Red, take her back to her room and lock her up."

"I can find it," she murmured, and hurried ahead of Red McLaglen.

"Rather good running shot, I'd say," the duke said in his proud, purring voice. "Neck bone always best unless you want to play with the game."

"I prefer shooting upland birds myself." Judge Chamberlain's voice came clearly to Clint's ears. "Of course, you need dogs for it."

"We like beaters of the human variety," the duke said. "They train easier, don't y'know?"

"I'm hungry," came Ralston's rough voice, and the men passed into the great lodge, comparing the merits of poached trout, buffalo hump roast, pheasant under glass, and stuffed venison hearts.

Clint heard the duke say, "Post the guard, Tony," and Douglas reply, "Right you are, Your Lordship."

Clint backed to the side door and went down to the basement hallway.

Bound to be a way up to the kitchen, he thought, trying different locked doors as he walked along the hall.

It wasn't a door, it was simply another stairway that came down from the right.

He heard voices coming from the kitchen, the chef's high-pitched exclamations overriding all.

Where would the judge have put his travel case? Surely not in the dining room. It seemed more natural to Clint that it would be in the library.

Backtracking swiftly, he hurried outside and around to the rear of the lodge to the window he'd entered the first time.

Raising his head slowly, he saw the room was empty and, pressing his thumbs on the wooden crosspieces, quietly raised the window.

Dropping inside to his knees, he waited but heard no footsteps. Then he rose to his feet, grateful for the cushion of the buffalo robe on the floor.

The brown calfskin bag sat close to the door, appearing as if the judge had opened the door, slid the bag inside, then gone out to the veranda to have a drink and enjoy the sport.

Lifting the bag, Clint turned back toward the window and saw the gun barrel, the red-mottled hand, and the face of Red McLaglen grinning at him through the open window.

"Come along, cowboy," McLaglen said triumphantly, "the gents want to run you this afternoon."

Clint flung the bag at him as McLaglen fired, his bullet tearing harmlessly through Clint's shirtsleeve.

Drawing quickly, Clint snapped a shot that drove splinters into McLaglen's eyes, making him miss again.

Clint's quick second shot punched a dark red hole between McLaglen's red eyebrows, and the big Irishman fell like a loose-jointed length of chain.

Reloading quickly, Clint grabbed the bag and started for the window as he heard the pounding of boots in the hall.

Backing off to one side, his six-gun at the ready, he heard Tony Douglas howl, "He's inside."

"Blast him out!" roared Big Jim Ralston, and suddenly the locked door was rocked by muzzle blasts and lead slugs smashing it open.

"Around back!" the duke snapped, and still Clint waited patiently as a hunter in a stand.

From the hall he heard angry men arguing, giving orders, jostling, pushing, and Doc Snordt's whimpering.

Outside, Tony Douglas ducked down below the window.

When Clint snapped a shot at the middleweight, the doctor was suddenly shoved into the room, screaming, "Not me! Not me!"

Clint held back from firing and the doctor slid to his knees, facing Clint, his hands held together in an attitude of prayer. "Please . . . ," he gasped, tears leaking down his pale face, his mustache twitching. "I didn't do anything . . ."

A shot from the hall, and a heavy rifle slug broke the doctor's lower leg, the impact hurling him into the corner.

Clint fired rapidly through the open door, then quickly reloaded the empty chambers.

"Drop your gun," the duke's voice purred from the hall, "and we'll make you a deal."

"You're not runnin' me," Clint yelled back, keeping his eyes on the open window where Tony Douglas likely would be waiting just below.

"It's a standoff," came the voice of Big Jim Ralston. "Leave the bag and you can ride away free."

After a long pause, Clint said weakly, "All right . . . I'll leave the bag. Don't shoot!"

"Don't worry, my word is good. Come right on out."

Clint picked up a buckskin-covered bolster from the couch, eased over toward the door, and said, "All right, here I come."

Clint tossed the bolster through the door, and the walls shook from a fusillade of rifles, shotguns, and six-shooters.

Tony Douglas poked his head up quickly and Clint fired; the bullet, off track, plowed a gouge across Tony's left cheek, and he dropped with a scream of pain.

Not hesitating, Clint leaped like a wildman to the doorway, fired blindly down the hall, and heard agonized responses as he retreated back into the library and ran to the open window.

Douglas knelt, the palm of his left hand jammed against the side of his face, his six-gun pointed but not aimed at the window.

Douglas's instinctive shot came first but missed, and Clint's return shot broke through Douglas's mouth, killing him almost instantly.

Another shot thundered from the doorway, stinging Clint's left arm, and he threw himself behind the couch as the duke leaned in the doorway with an engraved shotgun belching smoke, flame, and a dozen double-ought buckshot.

Clint felt the sharp pain in his dragging left leg and flopped on the floor as the second barrel blew a hole through the couch just above his head.

Rising to his knees, Clint fired into the smoke, blindly aiming for what he hoped was the doorway.

He heard a cough and the sound of a heavy weapon falling to the floor, then the Duke of Dorset slowly staggered out from the pall of smoke and pitched to the floor.

The duke's right hand clutched his bleeding paunch, and he coughed again like a dying billy goat.

Clint came to his feet with his smoke-blackened features transformed by revenge and raw survival.

Crabbing to the door, he showed his hat, but there was no response and he stepped into the hall ready for battle.

Nothing.

Hurrying, without thinking of the pain in his leg or arm, he came to the great hall where the dining room table was set with crystal goblets, Limoge porcelain, and great silver platters filled with still-steaming delicacies.

Standing at the head of the table, his trembling hands held high, Judge Chamberlain cried out, "Don't shoot! I'm not armed!"

"Where's Ralston?" Clint demanded, ready

to destroy his betrayer just to vent his red smoking rage.

"Gone for help," the judge said quickly. "I'm on your side now that I've learned the truth."

"I wouldn't trust you if you were on fire," Clint said, glancing toward the door opened to the veranda.

"He'll get away!" the judge warned.

"Stand there and don't move," Clint snapped, lowering his .44 and limping toward the open door.

"Trust me," the judge said.

Clint heard the tinge of mockery in the voice and dropped flat to the floor as a bullet screamed over his head.

Turning, he saw gunsmoke clouding the judge's right hand as a second small-caliber slug from the hideaway pistol needled through his left hip.

Without hesitating, Clint drove a heavy soft-nosed bullet through the judge's bowels before the judge could fire a third time.

Not pausing, Clint lurched out to the veranda and caught sight of Big Jim Ralston running across the bare yard toward the bunkhouse.

Clint pulled the trigger, but the hammer fell on an empty chamber.

Dropping the six-gun, he grabbed up one

of the Big Fifties leaning against the wall, levered in a huge cartridge, sighted in the right shoulder of the giant man, and fired. The 700-grain bullet smashed through his shoulder blade, slamming Ralston down on his face.

The big man got to his feet, looked fearfully over his left shoulder, and lumbered on toward the bunkhouse.

Clint slowly sighted in his left hip, squeezed, and blew it to pieces.

The big man collapsed. Clint eased down the stairs, levering in another brass-cased cartridge.

Hobbling across the yard to where he could face Big Jim Ralston, he waited until Ralston lifted his heavy torso up with his left arm and stared into Clint's eyes.

Sweat made muddy rivulets down the broad, hard-lined face as Ralston's eyes bulged with the effort to hold himself up.

"No more, cowboy," Ralston groaned. "I'll give you anything you want — just help me."

"I'm goin' to help you, big man. Same as you helped my little brother," Clint muttered.

A racking cough convulsed Ralston's body. His left arm gave way, the hand plowing a furrow in the dirt, and the left side of his head eased down to rest on the arm. Clotting blood oozed from the corner of his mouth, but he kept his eyes on Clint kneeling beside him.

"Got a bone splinter tearin' up your lung, big man. Want me to put you outa your misery?" Clint said, lifting the rifle barrel and placing the muzzle against the broad florid forehead.

"Go ahead," Ralston rasped, painfully gasping for breath and staring up the blue steel barrel into Clint's unflinching eyes.

"Please . . . mercy . . ."

"Reckon not," Clint said, shaking his head and laying the rifle aside. "Likely Lee would want equal justice for all. I hope you make it to trial."

"Finish it," the big man coughed, a rising tide of blood slobbering from his contorted lips, "the pain . . . too much . . . the pain!"

"I want you alive," Clint said.

Ralston's face suffused with hatred, his eyes bulged madly as he bared his teeth like a gutshot wolf dying in agony.

Clint turned his head and gazed quietly off at the rolling green hills everlasting.

"Out of my way!" the big man ranted from another world before strangling on his own blood.

Slump-shouldered, Clint got to his feet and looked up at the knoll where his brother lay. He took a deep breath and murmured, "Finally there's justice, there's peace, and there's the long night. Sleep well. . . ."

Taking another steadying breath, Clint stared up at the knoll and added softly, "I been growin' up just like you wanted, little brother, but where did the old clown go?"

# CHAPTER 14

Most of the out-of-town journalists had voted for the Calico Queen Saloon, although a few leaned toward the Buffalo. Some of the town ladies thought Doctor Snordt's big house would be a more genteel meeting place, but Ruby Campbell sent word she and Norah Kitt were coming, and as there was no one in town willing to stop them, it was agreed that the schoolhouse would serve as the first town hall of Sawtooth.

Reporters and correspondents clad in wrinkled suits and smelling of rum sat at the benches and desks, mingling with the townspeople.

Norah Kitt and Ruby Campbell were squired to the hall by two veteran writers who had been quick to discover nauchtown in their quest for local color.

Sitting behind the teacher's desk, facing the assemblage, were Emily Smith, Clint Durby, Lafe Nofziger, and Badger Corbin, all dressed in simple daily wear. Badger Corbin's shoulder was neatly bandaged and Clint Durby's left arm was suspended in a clean white sling.

The gangly Nofziger looked over the room and rapped on the desk with a ceramic ink bottle until the room was silent and waiting expectantly.

"Ladies and gentlemen," Nofziger croaked nervously, his Adam's apple going up and down like a bouncing ball, "we're here to clear up the whole mess that happened last week out at Sawtooth ranch. You newspaper folks are welcome and we hope you'll see that Sawtooth is a prosperous, growing city with a great future and not just a —"

"— slaughterhouse," a reporter in a checked suit and mousy sideburns put in.

"— mess of government corruption," another correspondent growled.

"No . . ." Nofziger wiped his pale, bony forehead with a red bandanna, "I'd call it a nice, homey place where the people stand up for law and order, and let the chips fall where they may. . . ."

Members of the press scribbled notes on wads of flimsy paper as Nofziger continued.

"I'm the new sheriff and my name is Lafe Nofziger, spelled N-O-F-Z-I-G-E-R, and I've collected all the evidence and know all the facts —"

"John Ripplewood of the *New York World*," a burly man in a yellowish suit with purple checks called out. "Were you present at the scene of the Sawtooth slaughter?"

"I was close by, riding hard to get there and take charge, but the only people left alive were these three at the table," Nofziger replied.

"What was your position there, ma'am? Tell us what you saw of the battle," asked a gnome of a reporter from London's *Pall Mall Gazette*.

"I was personal secretary to Senator Cooley," Emily said, her hand unconsciously wandering over to touch Clint's arm for support, "but when I discovered the nature of business the three men were conducting, I tried to leave. They restrained me, and I saw only the latter part of the action when Mr. Durby released me from captivity."

"Archie Bess, *St. Louis Globe*," a tall, clean-shaven reporter called out. "What started them fighting among themselves?"

"They never trusted one another, and after they had murdered Lee Durby, they feared each other all the more," Emily Smith said convincingly. "The actual fight came over the division of the spoils from their ongoing theft of public lands."

There was a pause as the reporters quickly made their notes and quotes.

"James Owensby, *New Orleans Picayune*. You there with the bandage, what did you see?"

"My name's Badger Corbin." Badger glared at the dude in the pinstriped suit. "I was in the bunkhouse and didn't see nothin'."

"Jack Bernier, *Boston Herald*," a short, round man dressed in a rumpled green-and-brown-striped suit spoke up. "Sheriff Nofziger, would you tell us what happened?"

"As I see it, they was drinking at the dinner table and arguin' about splittin' up the Crow Indian Reservation when Judge Chamberlain took a shot at somebody, and somebody shot him. I'm sure of that. One bunch run outside, the others forted up inside. They went at it like hellions until they was all dead."

"What was your part in this, mister?" the *Harper's* correspondent asked quickly, turning to Clint.

"Not much" — Clint shrugged — "but the real hero was my brother, Lee Durby. He discovered the Sawtooth Cattle Syndicate was really in the business of stealing great chunks of public and Indian land, and he was deliberately murdered by the kingpins before he could get loose to write the story."

"How did he uncover the scandal?" the *Gazette* reporter asked.

"He believed the press had the power to keep the rest of us honest," Clint said. "He figured you boys, more than lawmen, politicians, judges, soldiers, or church people, could keep things open and aboveboard."

"What was his name again?" the young reporter asked, his pencil poised.

"Lee Durby — spelled with a *u*," Clint murmured. "Just put down, 'Lee Durby, freelance reporter.' He'd appreciate that."

We hope you have enjoyed this Large Print book. Other Thorndike Press or Chivers Press Large Print books are available at your library or directly from the publishers. For more information about current and upcoming titles, please call or write, without obligation, to:

Thorndike Press
P.O. Box 159
Thorndike, Maine 04986
USA
Tel. (800) 223-6121 (U.S. & Canada)
In Maine call collect: (207) 948-2962

*OR*

Chivers Press Limited
Windsor Bridge Road
Bath BA2 3AX
England
Tel. (0225) 335336

All our Large Print titles are designed for easy reading, and all our books are made to last.